Gifts to the Prodigal

D to the Fourth Books & Scripts, LLC

ISBN: 979-8-9917233-1-2

D to the Fourth Books & Scripts, LLC

Stanley, NC

United States of America

To Pastor Brian Elwell, whose messages inspire me on a regular basis. One of your messages, in particular, provided inspiration for this story. Thank you.

Table of Contents

Gifts to the Prodigal

Dewey Dellinger

Chapter One

Earl Stanley, dressed in his pulpit robe and stole, surveyed the congregation from behind the pulpit. He was in his element. One recent religious magazine named him as one of the nation's top and most charismatic preachers, even though he wasn't at a megachurch. That's really where he wanted to be. The church of which he was pastor was a large church, but it wasn't a megachurch, and it didn't have a televised ministry available to viewers nationwide, which was what he desperately sought. Even his name was a good name for a preacher. There were lots of well-known preachers named Earl, and he shared his last name with the late Charles Stanley, no relation. In his mid-thirties, and with his popularity and moderate good looks, he believed there was nowhere to go but up the ladder.

Too bad he was a fraud! Not in any scandalous sense, and he definitely wasn't one of those preachers who promised healing or favor from God for an ongoing donation as proof of faith. He believed what he preached, and he believed in the Apostle's Creed. Still, he was a fraud, and he had been for quite some time, not as a preacher but as a pastor. He didn't start out that way after finishing seminary over twelve years ago. In fact, he wasn't that great of a preacher to begin with, but what he had been great at was community outreach. That was his original calling and what drove him into the ministry in the first place. He had believed that the best way to show God's love was to reach out to those in need and meet them where they were. He didn't believe in badgering people to join his church. He had believed that people had to have their basic needs met and to see themselves as valuable and capable. People needed to believe in love before they could accept God's love. That was what he had been. Now he was just a preacher, someone who delivered a rousing sermon. He was no longer a genuine pastor who sought those in need; he quit being that nearly ten years ago. Oh, he performed the obligatory services that was expected of him, weddings and funerals, but that was about all.

Outside, the cold and dreary November landscape with its bare trees and leaves covering the ground like a ruffled blanket served as a subtle reminder that Christmas was around the corner. Although it wasn't the Advent Season yet, a period of four Sundays before Christmas, Earl was preaching a Christmas-themed message.

"So, when Joseph and Mary went on the ninety-mile journey to Bethlehem by foot or by donkey, they didn't know each other well. They didn't know there would be no room for them in the inn, and they didn't know King Herod would come after their baby, who had not yet been born. Imagine the doubts and fears that must have plagued them during this time. Yet in the midst of all of these unknowns, some ordinary and some extraordinary, God took care of them. And all along, they were part of a divine plan to bring hope and redemption to the world."

After the sermon, as was tradition, Earl greeted his parishioners as they left the church after the Sunday morning worship service. One of the parishioners, Ed Bowles, a medium-build man in his sixties with grayed and peppered hair, paused to chat. "Excellent sermon, as usual, pastor. When you go to the

Church Conference next week, I hope they let you stay here another year."

Earl smiled warmly at the compliment, but he said nothing in reply. The Church Conference was a regional conference the denomination held every year in November. The purpose of the Conference was severalfold. There were various sessions for pastors to attend, meetings where church doctrine was used to evaluate and to discuss modern trends, a time for reflection and renewal, and most importantly for Earl, a time when pastors found out their next church assignment. Usually, about every four years, pastors were reassigned to other churches, and Earl hoped and prayed that this year he would get his wish of pastoring a megachurch. That gave Earl an idea. Planting the seed with the bishop who worked with other bishops in making those assignments wouldn't hurt.

That night, Earl was in his parsonage, a nice modern house in a nice neighborhood. Housing was a benefit he had as a pastor that he didn't have to pay for; it was part of his salary and benefits package. Earl lived alone in the parsonage. He had never been married, and he wasn't dating anyone. If anything stood in his way of becoming a pastor at a megachurch, being unmarried might be that obstacle. Televised ministries, at least occasionally, liked to show the pastor's family and children, as if being a family man were some unwritten criterion of being a good pastor. Earl was in his study, his pastor cave, so to speak, which was lined with bookcases of various religious books, bibles, and concordances. On one wall was a framed magazine cover that proclaimed, *America's Up-and-Coming Ministers*. Earl was one of the featured ministers on the cover.

Earl pulled out his phone and found the contact number of the bishop, Christian Goodpaster. Honest to goodness, that was the bishop's name. You couldn't get a more Christian-sounding name than that. With a name like that, one almost had to be in the ministry. Besides being his current bishop, Bishop Goodpaster had been a seminary professor when Earl was in seminary, and Earl took several classes from him. After Bishop Goodpaster left the seminary to take an office as bishop, Earl had become good friends with the man, and now called him Chris, at least in private and social situations. Earl punched the icon on the phone, and Chris answered after a few rings.

"Hi, Chris. This is Earl."

"Good to hear from you Earl. I suppose you're calling about the Conference next week. I had a feeling I'd get a call from you."

"You're not getting divine revelations now, are you?"

"No," chuckled Chris. "It's more about knowing people and their personalities."

"Well, I won't play out that conversation any further; it sounds as though it might be embarrassing for me. Let me get to the point. I know we're going to discuss at the conference where my assignment will be next year, but I want to let you know that I'm ready for a megachurch assignment. I think a televised ministry will be a good way to share my gift."

"I've thought quite a bit about that recently. I'll have an answer for you next week."

"Alright. Thanks, Chris. See you next week."

Earl disconnected and laid the phone on his desk. He cast a glance at the full-length mirror in the room, which he used as an aid in observing his sermon delivery. He crept toward it with shame for the prideful feeling that swelled within him. He stood in front of it and peered deeply into it. Rather than seeing his reflection in the mirror, he imagined himself at the pulpit of a megachurch, standing confidently in his pulpit robe and stole with a slight smile on his face and gleaming as he surveyed his flock. The sea of congregants came from all walks of life. Some wore expensive suits or exquisite dresses. Others were in jeans and casual shirts. They had one thing in common; they were there to see him and to hear the inspiring message he had carefully crafted for them on that day. He saw his mannerisms, carefully choreographed to punctuate particular points of emphasis. He saw a myriad of reactions as people soaked up his words, inspiration on some faces, tears in the eyes of others, penitent expressions, and eagerness to leave the sanctuary and apply in their lives what they heard.

As his vision slowly faded, the man standing in the mirror told him it was only a hopeful daydream. The pang of guilt stung his conscience over his prideful indulgence. He felt silly, like a teenage boy looking in the mirror to see if his muscles had gotten bigger. He wondered if he was wrong for imagining the scene. He tried to justify his action as visualization of a goal he wanted. He told himself that faith was being certain that what one desired would actually happen, that what one didn't see actually exists. Faith was feeling like your desire had already been fulfilled. His visualization was a way of building faith. It was using his imagination to see his life as it would be, proof of the reality of his desire.

Fear entered his mind, telling him that maybe he didn't deserve it. He tried countering the fear. Preaching was what he was good at. It was his gift. Wouldn't God want him to use that gift to its fullest extent, to share God's message with others? Well, he had planted the seed with Chris. Hopefully, it would grow in Chris' mind and produce fruit.

Earl skulked away from the mirror, feeling as though he had been caught in some narcissistic indulgence. Some faith. But he supposed that building faith was much like building anything else. It took some time and some trial and error.

Chapter Two

"Good morning, Zola," chirped Earl as we walked into the church office early Monday morning.

"Good morning, Pastor Earl."

Zola always returned the greeting in a manner that Earl never knew quite how to take. She wasn't an easy read, and Earl joked with her occasionally that she would be a good poker player. The first time he told her that, she let him know right away that she had no vices that she knew of, and poker was definitely something she would not partake in. So, he used sparingly any comments about being a good poker player or having a poker face. Usually, he would only resort to that to raise her ire on some mischievous occasion.

Zola had been the church secretary for close to fifteen years, long before his arrival there. She was in her late thirties and good at what she did. Earl passed her desk without further conversation and went straight into his study. As soon as he entered his office, he sat behind his desk and went straight to work on next week's sermon. He had drafted it a couple of weeks before and wanted to put the finishing touches on it so that he could work on and hopefully get drafts of the sermons for the Advent season. The month or so before Christmas was always busy for people, getting exponentially more so the closer one got to Christmas. Although Earl didn't really have any shopping to do, since he had no living relatives, the activities around Christmas always seemed to harry people, and harried people were infectious, which they passed along causing others to be harried as well.

After about thirty minutes into working on his sermons, he had jotted down quite a bit of notes on a notepad. Zola walked into Earl's study carrying a folder. When she saw him writing, she made a "hmph" sound, causing Earl to look up.

"I don't know why you still resort to writing when there are so many different technological devises you could use that make things much easier for you," admonished Zola.

"I'm old fashioned when it comes to making outlines. I guess that's because there are so many different technologies to use." That was partly true. Earl liked the feel of a pencil or pen in his hand. The firmness of the writing instrument versus the yielding keys on laptop provided a comforting feeling. And he didn't like the recording option that software now provided. He tended to ramble, and going back and fixing it seemed to take as much time as it saved.

Zola approached his desk in her typical no-nonsense way and plopped the folder directly on top of his notepad. That's not subtle at all, thought Earl. The folder was labeled *Community Outreach Meeting*.

Just in case he needed to be reminded, "Don't forget the community outreach meeting this afternoon with the local pastors," Zola asserted.

Earl knew she said that in case he needed to be reminded. Actually, she probably knew he didn't need to be reminded, just needled. "I thought we were sending the associate pastor to that meeting."

"You thought wrong. The meeting is for pastors, not associate pastors. Besides, you, not we, already have her doing another outreach event in your place."

Zola was a mother of two children. No one could get anything by her, and sometimes, Earl thought she treated him like one of her children.

As Zola marched out of his study, Earl picked up the folder and shuffled through the pages before tossing it to the side on top of a pile of other papers and folders before returning to work on the sermons.

About an hour later, Zola interrupted Earl once again as she escorted Carl into his study. Carl was a church member whom Earl had cajoled into doing some volunteer work for him. The volunteer work as at Woodlawn, an alternative school for young teens who did not fit in for one reason or another at their assigned schools.

"Good morning, Pastor."

Although Earl was annoyed by another interruption, he tried not to display the annoyance on his face as he looked up from his work to greet Carl. "Good morning, Carl. What can I do for you?"

Carl wore a big grin across his face. "I'm really enjoying the opportunity you gave me to do volunteer work with the teens at Woodlawn."

"Good to hear," replied Earl matter-of-factly.

"One of the things we've noticed is that the youth have trouble with interpersonal communication, especially conflict resolution skills. With your speaking ability, I was hoping you could go with me one day and talk about or show some ideal ways to deal with conflict. I think that would help them a lot in everyday situations."

Earl momentarily froze at the thought. His mind quickly raced for reasons to avoid the invitation until it came up with something plausible and passable. "Well, Carl, I'm really busy this week, and next week is the conference. Talk with Zola about getting our associate pastor to go with you. She's really good at that sort of thing."

"Ok … but if you change your mind let me know. Have a good day." Disappointment tinged Carl's voice and palpably dripped from him, melting his smile into a puddle on the floor. He slowly turned and shuffled toward the door and out of the study.

As soon as Carl had turned around, Earl was back to his sermon notes. When he heard the door close, he looked up and sighed, trying to let as much guilt escape as possible. There wasn't enough sighing he could do though to let that much guilt escape his mind and body. He had preached a sermon one time of the symbolism of yeast in the Bible and how it represented sin. Guilt was the same. Guilt had a terrible way of expanding through one's body, mind, and soul. As it expanded, it transformed the very nature of the person into whom it had been injected. Like yeast, once it was baked in, it effused the bread. And once that transformation had taken place, undoing it was nearly impossible.

Earl became frustrated once more when Zola all but turned his chair over to get him up and out of his study to go the community center for the Community Outreach Meeting. When Earl reached the center, the room was filled with local pastors. Apparently, he was the last to arrive. Although the meeting had yet to begin, the large meeting room was filled with dozens of simultaneous discussions among groups of pastors about possible outreach activities. The outreach activities he had encountered today were like flies. He would bat them away, only for them to return to annoy him again.

Earl saw a folding chair that had not been set out that was leaning against a wall. Unnoticed, he took the chair and set it near the door at the back of the room. He purposely avoided entering any discussions with any of the other pastors and secretly hoped the meeting would start soon. The sooner it started, the sooner it would end, as long as no long-winded pastor was leading the event. As he waited for the meeting to begin, he studied the engagement of all the other pastors. He felt out of place, out of his element, and he desperately wanted to rush out through the door. He debated whether to go now or slog through the meeting. Just as his mind told him to flee, Reverend Baxter stood at the front of the room trying to hush the crowd.

Earl had forgotten that Reverend Baxter, who always seemed overly organized, overly energetic, and overly optimistic, was the leader of this group. Whatever the allotted time was for this meeting, Reverend Baxter would go over it by at least an hour. How could someone be so organized and still not stay within time limits?

"I'm hearing some great outreach ideas discussed, called out Reverend Baxter with what seemed like feigned enthusiasm. "Get into groups of three to five people. I would like each group to come up with their best feasible, outreach idea. I'll give you twenty minutes, and then we'll have someone from each group report out."

That was all Earl needed to hear. He didn't like group work. He didn't want to go around in a group with everyone stating their opinion, and he didn't want to risk being the one chosen to report out. As the groups began to form, Earl surreptitiously exited the building. Earl was on the walkway about halfway from the building to the parking lot when he heard someone call out his name. As he turned around, he saw Reverend Jung running up to him.

"Reverend Stanley, I've been trying to contact you for a while. World Children's Day is coming up soon, and I was hoping that our two churches, since they are two of the larger churches in the community, could partner to do an event. Perhaps a church fair where we have some games, different cultural activities, and educational booths for parents."

"I'm really busy, and I attend our annual Church Conference next week. Besides, I think it's too close to World Children's Day to organize a big event now."

"Last year, you said we would try to do something this year, and I've left messages for two months. Even if we do something small, I think we could still pull it off. I'm sure here are plenty of people who would happily help."

"I'm sorry, Reverend Jung. Maybe next year."

Reverend Jung appeared downcast. It showed in his face and in his hunched-over posture. Earl turned and walked hurriedly to the parking lot. He hoped that his fast pace wouldn't betray his eagerness to get away from the uncomfortable situation. Earl reached his car and glanced back toward the building. Reverend Jung was just going through the door back into the building. Earl felt as though he had dodged a bullet, but he had not dodged the guilt and shameful feeling that found him. The look on Reverend Jung's face guaranteed that.

Chapter Three

That night, Earl was at the home of Juan and Luciana Lopez. They were members of the church who had invited Earl for dinner. Both were in their mid to late thirties, and they had two children. Joaquin had recently turned ten years old, and his younger sister, Elena, was eight years old.

The dining room was warm and inviting and blended in touches of their Mexican heritage. A soft golden glow emanated from a wrought-iron chandelier hanging above the sturdy wooden dining room table. A colorful hand-woven table runner ran down the center of the table, displaying geometric patterns in vibrant hues of red, orange, and turquoise. On it sat bowls of guacamole and salsa with their vivid rich green and red colors that reminded Earl of Christmas. The walls were painted in a warm terracotta hue and were adorned with decorative hand-painted tiles, a woven tapestry, and family photographs. The warm atmosphere complemented the meal on the table. The savory aromas of marinated pork and grilled corn filled the air. Earl offered a quick prayer, eager to indulge in a meal that so saturated his nose.

"We're having Tacos al Pastor in honor of you, Pastor," beamed Luciana.

Earl smiled at the play on words honoring him. "Everything smells so delicious that I can't wait to enjoy what you all have prepared."

"It was a family effort; everyone helped, and we had fun doing it," shared Luciana.

Earl wondered if this was a veiled hint to his marital status and what he was missing out on. He didn't like jumping immediately to that conclusion, but his experience had biased him toward that direction.

As they prepared the tacos, the scent of spices, pineapple, cilantro, and limes wafted through the air mixing with the smell of the soft corn tortillas. Earl's mouth watered as he anticipated biting into the flavorful taco. In addition to the Tacos al Pastor and elote were frijoles charros and a jicama and orange salad.

As Earl was finishing his third taco, Juan asked, "Do you think they'll let you stay here another year?"

Earl swallowed the last bite and wondered how he had eaten so much as he prepared to answer Juan's question. "The Conference usually changes pastors every three to four years," explained Earl. "I've been here four years. I imagine I will be sent to another church in July."

We hope you can stay another year," stressed Luciana, "but we understand that you have to go where God sends you. Just know that you will be missed greatly."

"Thank you, Luciana. Wherever I'm sent, I doubt anyone's cooking will come close to yours." Earl meant it without any doubt.

"Are you getting ready for Christmas?" probed Luciana.

"I have the outlines of my sermons already laid out."

"No. Are you ready for Christmas?" reiterated Luciana, emphasizing the word *ready*.

"Well, it's just me; so, I have no big plans," answered Earl casually.

Elena, who had been quiet for the most part up to this point, asked Earl a pointed question. "Why don't you help with the Christmas activities?"

Juan's eyes widened temporarily before returning to normal, and he looked directly at Elena as he admonished her. "Elena. That's not a polite question to ask a guest."

"Why not?" she responded innocently.

At this point, her older brother attempted to answer her question. "Because it puts him on the defensive."

Elena scrunched up her face in a confused look. "What's that?"

She certainly was a curious girl, thought Earl.

Joaquin shrugged his shoulders. "We learned that word in school last week, but I don't know what sports has to do with it."

This time Luciana jumped into the conversation. Earl suspected that she would have a try at explaining mealtime etiquette since Juan and Joaquin and not been successful. "Children! Behave or Pastor Earl may not come back anymore."

Earl squirmed in his seat, feeling guilty that Elena was taking all of the heat on his behalf. "That's ok." Earl directed his attention to Joaquin and Elena to try to reassure them that he had not been offended by their questions and comments. "Jesus loved children because they get right to the point. *Defensive* is like sports. What does the defense do?"

Joaquin was like a kid in school who eagerly wanted to answer the teacher's question. His face beamed, and he squirmed in his seat with excitement. He all but raised his hand. "They try to keep the other team from scoring, and they try to take the ball away."

Earl stifled a chuckle at the enthusiasm in which Joaquin answered. "That's right." A slight smile formed on Earl's face. "Very good. When a person is defensive, it means they try to keep someone's words from hurting them and they try to take the conversation back from the other person."

"Oh!" exclaimed Joaquin drawing out the word and looking pensively toward the ceiling. "I wish the teacher would have explained it that way. How do you know so much about sports?"

Earl leaned in toward Joaquin as he answered. "The church I pastored before coming here was near Atlanta, and I had a professional basketball player, Jarrett Bridges, in the congregation. He plays for Philadelphia now."

Joaquin's eyes grew wide, and his mouth dropped open. "Wow! He's great! Did you get his autograph?"

"In fact, I have an autographed basketball he gave me."

"Wow!" Joaquin was still wide-eyed and open-mouthed.

Elena folded her arms and wore a pouty face. "The pastor never answered my question."

She's curious and persistent. That's quite a combination, thought Earl. "Well, Elena, I have an associate pastor who helps with all of that. I used to do all sorts of activities with people, but I mostly preach now."

"Why did you stop?"

This young girl could put Socrates to the test, thought Earl as he started to become slightly uncomfortable now at her continued questioning. He felt like he was in school undergoing a heavy dose of Socratic questioning. "Well ... er ... Let's just say that I tried doing outreach, but my talent was in another area."

"Did other people help you?" she continued.

At least this wasn't a *why* question. "No. I did it on my own."

Elena scrunched her eyebrows together and had a faraway look in her eyes as though she were getting ready to say something profound. Earl squirmed some more as she slowly began to formulate her thought into words. "So, you did ... reach out ... on your own. You preach on your own. You're not married. Do you always do everything by yourself?"

The exhaled breath through Earl's nose made a slight sound, and the corners of his mouth turned down slightly. "I guess I never thought of it that way." And he hadn't. This young girl was like a therapist who diagnosed him in a few minutes of something, that for years, he had not seen in himself.

Seemingly emboldened by Earl's answer, Elena offered more of her wisdom. "Mama says that you can accomplish something by yourself, but it's better when people work together."

At this point, Luciana threw her napkin on the table, squinted her eyes at Elena, and puffed out her lips. "Elena, stop right now!" Luciana timidly glanced at Earl with a much different facial expression than the look she had just given Elena. "I'm sorry, Pastor."

Earl interjected before she could continue to apologize further, "That's quite alright. She conveyed more in a few sentences than I sometimes do in an entire sermon." He smiled widely to show there were no hard feelings.

The smile seemed to put Luciana at ease, and she relaxed her shoulders releasing the tension that Earl had not noticed until now. "You're good with children. If you are sent somewhere else, I hope you can find someone there and start a family."

Earl forced a smile. He had thought he had avoided that subject. It was a subject that surfaced like clockwork every time he was at a social gathering with members of his congregation. He never knew what to say. He had just not met the right woman for him. Maybe he was too picky, but as an ordained reverend, he didn't want to enter into marriage lightly, or any romantic relationship lightly for that matter.

Chapter Four

That night, as Earl slept, he began to squirm and toss in his bed. His head moved from side to side as if trying to avoid looking at something he was seeing in his nightmare.

A younger Earl stood in the church boardroom, like an accused defendant, in front of a group of Church Council Leaders. The seven-member group of church leaders were all older stern-faced men. Richard Coldwell was the head lay leader. He was in his fifties and was a descendant of one of the founding families of the church. He was an authoritarian leader, a traditionalist, and was the self-appointed guardian of the church's legacy. Richard was angry to the point of being hysterical. He looked as though he were Satan accusing humankind, red-faced and scowling with an outstretched arm and pointed finger. His words were harsh and biting, penetrating the toughest armor into the very core of a person. Earl quivered at his presence.

"In one year," accused Richard, spittle spewing out of his mouth as he pointed and glared at Earl, "you've ruined a church that has almost a three-hundred-year-old history. The Council has voted to terminate your pastorship of Pinewood Church.

We've called the bishop and asked him to appoint another pastor. We demand your resignation immediately. I swear if it's the last thing I do, I'll make sure you never serve another church again."

Earl awoke in the pitch dark in a cold sweat, trembling from the nightmare, a nightmare that was a recurring one. His whole body was tense, and his chest felt tight. The knot in his throat wouldn't budge as he forcefully tried to swallow it, and he gasped, hoping for just one lungful of fresh air. Earl never knew when the nightmare would decide to pop up. At one point, he went a year or more without having it. Another year, he had it three times. Every time he had it, he felt as though he were going through his own private emotional hell. Tormented by the nightmare and afraid to go back to sleep else he fall back into it, Earl slept very little the rest of the night.

Chapter Five

A week had passed, and Earl was at the Church Conference. This year, the conference was at a retreat in the mountains of North Carolina. The retreat set on over one thousand acres with a lake occupying approximately two hundred acres. There was a conference center along with an on-site hotel and cabins and outdoor activities. In November, walking trails was about the extent of the activities that anyone participated in. The Church Conference ran from Monday through Friday. Concurrent sessions were offered, covering a variety of topics. A few plenary sessions were scheduled, featuring prominent speakers. Other sessions were held to adopt future goals, to discuss programming and budgeting, and to discuss the church's position on modern-day issues and trends. Time was also built in for personal reflection and social activities. And of course, this was the time that pastors found out if they would stay at their current church or change churches come July.

On Monday, Earl presented at one of the concurrent sessions on how to deliver an effective sermon. He attended one other concurrent session and the plenary session on peacebuilding in a polarized world. Earl was antsy though because his appointment with the bishop to find out his next church assignment was the next day. To calm himself, Earl took a two-hour walk along the trails. Earl dressed in the one set of the few comfort clothes he brought. He wore a lumberjack-looking, red flannel shirt, a pair of cargo pants and a pair of hiking shoes. He attached a water bottle to his belt and put a small Bible into one of the cargo pockets.

The November air in the mountains was cold, invigorating, and just a tad biting. As Earl walked, he quickly warmed up enough not to notice the cold. At first, the trail meandered lazily through a forest of oaks and pines. Nature's symphony, the sounds of chirping birds and the rustling of small unseen animals in the forest, greeted his ears. The scent of pine and the earthy decay of leaves grounded him in the present moment. Earl had been here in the summer when the oaks and other hardwoods were at their fullest with leaves. The contrast in the winter was somewhat striking, but the forest still seemed dense enough with all of the interspersed evergreens. The sun peeped from behind a cloud, displaying a dappled patchwork of light and shadows on the path before him. As the trail ascended, it no longer meandered but rose at a brisk pace, and the pines yielded somewhat to hardwoods: oak, hickory, and poplars. The trail that had been covered by soft pine needles or bare spots of soft damp earth was now rocky and filled with thick roots. Clouds rolled in, covering the sun and creating a dismal-looking day. As the narrow path reached the summit, Earl found a large rock and sat to rest before the trail began its descent.

Earl pulled the small Bible out of his pocket and opened it to random page. He felt peace descend upon him and penetrate into his being. Closing his eyes, he inhaled the sharp air into his lungs. He exhaled his cares and worries and felt one with his surroundings. Earl prayed, thanking God for allowing him to partake in the peace and beauty of the Master Architect's creation.

He ended his prayer with a request that he receive the church appointment he wanted, but he added that God's will be done.

Feeling refreshed, Earl began the descent of the trail loop. Eventually the steep narrow path returned to a meandering trail. He spotted a fox at one point that stared at him for a moment before turning and going its way. Several minutes later, he came across a deer; it startled upon seeing him and bounded gracefully through the trees.

The trail eventually paralleled a small stream of slow-moving water. Within a few hundred feet the stream picked up its pace as it rushed over rocks. The stream widened where the trail crossed it, and Earl crossed using the large rocks rising above the water's surface. Earl paused to admire the natural beauty of his surroundings, and he wished he could sit in a spot all day just soaking it all in. The sun had dipped low in the sky though, escaping the confines of the clouds. As long shadows were cast across his path, he reluctantly picked up his pace until he entered the clearing and the buildings and cabins of the retreat grounds.

Tuesday morning, Earl eagerly made his way to meet the bishop in one of the offices in the conference center. A temporary name plate above one of the office doors read *Bishop Christian Goodpaster*. The door was open, and Earl saw the bishop sitting behind a desk studying a document. The scene reminded Earl of visiting his former professor in his office at seminary. Now, instead of essays piled in front of him waiting to be graded, he had a list of church appointments. The bishop was obviously older looking than he had been when he served as a professor. He was in his late fifties now. A few more lines etched his face, but he still appeared young and vibrant. Rather than barging directly into the office, Earl politely knocked on the door frame.

The bishop looked up at the sound, and a smile spread across his face. "Earl! Good to see you. Please come in." He rose from his chair and met Earl halfway in the small office and extended his hand.

Earl shook the bishop's hand with a smile matching that of the bishop. "Good to see you too, Chris."

"I hope you're enjoying the Conference."

"It's always good to be here, and it's always good to see my old seminary professor."

"I'm starting to resemble that remark, the part about being old. Don't say anything. I know I was never known for my sense of humor."

"But you were known for your tough classes. It was for sure that they were no joke. I never understood why you left your teaching job at the seminary."

Chris motioned for Earl to take a seat, and Chris sat in a chair facing Earl. "Just because God calls you to do a job, doesn't mean that is the one and only job God will always have you do. Sometimes, God calls you to do another job, something you weren't expecting." Realization seemed to set in on Chris' face that each appointment was set for a limited amount of time. "As much as I would like to reminisce about the old seminary days, I know our appointment is brief, and I'm sure you want to know where you will minister when the new appointments begin the first of July."

Earl took the opening to reiterate his desire. "I was hoping to be moved to one of the megachurches in Texas that has a televised ministry. Since preaching is perhaps my greatest gift, I feel that is where I can be the most beneficial. Have you thought about my request?"

Chris leaned back in the chair and stretched before answering Earl. "I must admit that you are one of the best I've ever seen when it comes to effective sermons. You read the scripture, provide a memorable vignette, get your three points in succinctly, and end with a good summary, all in fifteen to twenty minutes. And the chapter you wrote for the book the seminary uses for its *Delivering an Effective Sermon* course is the best guide I've seen."

Earl took this as a good sign and continued to press his case. "That's why I feel a church with a televised ministry will best utilize my gift."

"You know that when we place ministers, we take into consideration the pastor's request, but I pray over every placement."

To Earl, Chris seemed to be in his previous role as a professor, setting up a concept for the class to think critically about. The class would then study and discuss the concept. It also seemed to Earl that Chris was buying time. "Why do I feel there is a *but* coming up?"

Chris showed no reaction to Earl's comment, and he continued as if Earl had not asked the question. "Do you remember earlier?" prompted Chris. "I said that sometimes God calls you to do another job, something you weren't expecting."

Was this statement foreshadowing something to come? "Yes," replied Earl with a hint of trepidation in his voice.

"The pastor in a small town recently died. It was sudden and unexpected, and we need someone to fill in over the next six months. Since you are not married and don't have children, you would be the ideal candidate."

Earl's smile had vanished by this point. In its place was a tight thin line covering clenched teeth. Earl loosened the tension in his jaws enough to allow him to speak. "You're stalling, Chris. That's never a good sign. Am I being punished because I don't have a family? I know the pastors in these megachurches usually have the picture-perfect families, but I still have a lot to draw on even without a wife and children."

A barely audible sigh issued from Chris, as if he expected pushback from Earl and was now reaping the fruits of that expectation. "You're not being punished. We have a retirement coming up at a church in Dallas, Texas that I will give you in July. You'll get your wish, but I want you to fill in at this other church temporarily. We'll make sure that your current church is in good hands in the meantime."

Earl's forehead creased with concern, and an anxious feeling flooded his gut. "Where is the church you want me to fill in?" The question was slow and forced.

Chris rushed through the answer. "It's in Pinewood."

Earl wasn't sure he heard correctly; so, he tried to confirm it. Again, the words came out slow and forced. "Pine ... Pinewood ... as in Pinewood, Kentucky near the Kentucky, Tennessee, and Virginia borders?"

"That's right. I prayed over this numerous times, and every time, God gave me the same answer."

Earl turned his head slightly to the side, as if focusing out of one eye might reveal this whole discussion to be some prank, but Chris' face seemed unmoved. Surely the man in front of him hadn't become senile. "You can't be serious, Chris." Earl looked at Chris with pleading eyes. "Please. I beg you, not Pinewood." Earl didn't like begging. He hoped that something would register with Chris to help him realize his mistake.

"I know that was your first church out of seminary twelve years ago and that you had a rough time there, but you've successfully pastored other churches since then."

Earl wasn't sure he could trust what his ears were telling him. Earl wondered if he was asleep and if his nightmare was ready to start at any moment. He could feel the cold sweat begin to break out on his forehead, and his throat began to constrict. He had to talk while he still could. "Rough time? I came close to leaving the ministry after pastoring that church. It's been about eleven years since I left, but the thought of that time still haunts me to this day. If I had pastored the church two hundred years ago, I swear they would have tarred and feathered me and run me out of town on a rail. Please don't send me back there." Earl could hear the begging and pleading in his voice. Although he didn't like begging, if that was what it would take to change Chris' mind, he wasn't beyond begging. He looked at the stone face of Chris, but his pleading had not seemed to alter Chris' decision in the least. As a former professor, Chris was probably impervious to begging. It was something he had endured during his tenure and must have faced on a semester-to-semester basis. Earl could have kicked himself for not knowing better.

"Earl, we've been friends a long time, and you were one of the best students I had in seminary; so, let me be honest with you. You came back from that church a broken man. Sure, your sermons are great, but preaching wasn't your original gift; outreach was, and it came so easy for you."

"I do more than just preach. I officiate weddings and funerals."

"But when was the last time you went out and met your flock where they are? When you started in the ministry, you believed your purpose was to help people in the community who needed help. Surely you must remember that if I do, and we both know when that happened. You lost all of your confidence when it comes to outreach ministry. We didn't have a name for it then, but we call it imposter syndrome now. To be honest, you've become a preacher rather than a pastor."

Earl didn't know if Chris had intended the last line to be an insult or not. It certainly felt like an insult. Chris' honesty hit home, and it hit hard. Earl couldn't deny what Chris said, but Earl had come to terms with it. Why stir something up that didn't need to be stirred up? Why did this seem so important to Chris? It seemed more important to Chris than it did to Earl. Pinewood had been the most painful experience of his life. Earl wanted to flee Chris' office, and he rose from his chair. At the same time, he didn't want to give in without a fight. "Pinewood is a smaller church than the one I pastor now. This still feels like a punishment."

Chris' demeanor remained steadfast. "You need to come to peace with this episode from your past and round out your abilities if you're ever to move forward as a servant of God. God doesn't always do the easy things."

"God, or you?" Earl felt guilt-ridden for the last snarky remark. It was a cheap shot. He was defensive, and his thoughts drifted to the conversation he had with Joaquin about being defensive and trying to regain control of the conversation.

Chris didn't blink at Earl's remark. Maybe he had even expected it. "Pray over this, Earl. I think you know in your heart, it's for your own good."

Earl barely remembered eating the meal in the conference center dining hall that night. Was it chicken? It was usually chicken at these events. It was probably chicken. Or was it lasagna? Earl's thoughts had been on nothing else but his upcoming assignment. Sure, he was going to get his wish to serve at the megachurch in Dallas with a televised ministry, but he had to get through the six-month sentence at Pinewood. It was like purgatory before paradise.

Chris had suggested he pray over the assignment, and that's all he knew he could do. He certainly didn't want to compare himself to Jesus in any way, but he was reminded of the Garden of

Gethsemane. Jesus had asked that the cup be removed from which he was about to drink, referring to the crucifixion. Nevertheless, he asked that God's will be done. The Pinewood church was the cross that Earl didn't want to bear. As he kneeled by the bed, he fervently and earnestly prayed that he not be sent to Pinewood. Reluctantly, he asked that God's will be done, even though he didn't really mean it.

Chapter Six

Earl had another dream that night. It wasn't the nightmare from the other night, but he was once again the pastor of Pinewood Church. The events he dreamed were real events that had happened, and they played before his eyes like a montage in a movie.

He was at a mobile home park that was in close proximity to Pinewood Church. The younger version of himself was showing a raggedy-clothed boy how to play some chords on a guitar. He showed him the first few chords of the song, *Come to the Church in the Wildwood*. The sound of the chords strained the ear, but the youth kept at it until he could play the first few bars of the song. Earl held out his arm and hand in a *stop* motion when the boy started to hand Earl the guitar. Earl told him to keep it, and the kid gave a big, toothy smile as he ran his hand over the guitar, feeling its material and shape.

In the next scene of the dream, Earl was standing at the front of a room full of senior citizens as each huddled over bingo cards. Earl cranked the handle, spinning the steel cage containing the numbered balls. He opened the cage, grabbed a ball, and called out the number. In the middle of the room, a feeble-looking gray-haired woman enthusiastically cried out *Bingo* in a raspy voice as loudly as she could. Her smile revealed a few missing teeth. Although she had a walker, she got up from her seat on her own. Earl jogged toward her with her prize. It was some dollar-store item, but the woman held it up as if she had just won the Kentucky Derby trophy.

Next, Earl was at a soup kitchen. Some of the people were homeless. Others were just seeking a cooked meal. The smell of the soup could not cover up the smell of unwashed bodies and unwashed old clothes that were torn or literally unravelling. The dirt was almost a permanent feature of their faces that no amount of scrubbing could remove. Earl ladled steaming soup into a bowl that was held in shaking hands that came either from cold weather or poor health. The group was silent, except for the slurping and the clinking and scraping of spoons against the ceramic bowls.

The scene of the soup kitchen quickly changed, and now, Earl was outside on a bright sunny day. Even though he wore a baseball cap, his eyes squinted from the afternoon sun on the summer day. In a vacant field near the mobile home neighborhood, a makeshift baseball field had been hastily put up. Earl pitched easy pitches to the batters, calling balls rather than strikes as much as possible. Most had never played baseball, and Earl had brought numerous gloves and bats. The game was unorganized; but even with strikeouts, big hits, clean catches, missed catches, perfect throws, passable throws, overthrows, and argued calls of whether someone was safe or out, everyone seemed to have fun.

One of the girls who played baseball was limping heavily and apparently had twisted her ankle. Earl had brought a first-aid kit with him, and he showed the girl how to properly wrap her ankle.

Even though he was dreaming, he felt a warm sense of accomplishment, as if the things he was doing mattered. Suddenly, Earl began to fight with and kick the covers.

A dark billowing cloud covered the sun shining on the baseball field. Earl felt as though his body was transported. He had been summoned to the Pinewood Church meeting room one night. He stood before the seven-member group of church leaders, explaining his actions. "But as a church, we're commissioned to go out and help others, not just those in our congregation."

A scowl formed on Richard's face as he became irritated. By the time Earl had finished speaking, Richard had become red-faced. Earl could hear the tension and anger in Richard's voice as he spoke. "You were sent here to serve this church, not spend all of your time running around town, especially not spending so much time at that trailer park helping people who don't even go to church here."

"But it's the Christian thing to do." Earl stood his ground against Richard.

Richard stood up, putting his arms on the table and locking his elbows as he leaned forward. "We pay you to serve our congregation, and that's what you'll do, or we'll find someone who will."

Earl woke up from the beginning stages of the nightmare, before it turned even darker. Still, he was shaken. He sat up in bed and prayed. Enough of a peace settled on him to allow him to lie back down in bed. Within about ten minutes, he was asleep again.

Chapter Seven

The next morning, Earl sat across from Chris in Chris' makeshift office in the conference center. The previous day, Earl had tried pleading with Chris. He realized too late that pleading with a former professor, who faced that type of behavior constantly, was a losing cause. Today he was going to try a more rational approach. If anything would work against a former professor, that would. "Thanks for agreeing to see me again," began Earl. "I've been thinking and praying about this. It doesn't make sense to move me to cover a temporary position and get someone else to cover my current church on a temporary basis. Why not just have that person cover Pinewood? Is there not someone else you can send to Pinewood?"

Chris had apparently been prepared for this approach as well. He leaned back, crossed his arms, and fixed his gaze on Earl. "Do you recall Isaiah 6:8?"

Earl heaved a heavy sigh. He felt he was being given a pop quiz to see if he had memorized specific scriptures. From rote memory, he began quoting the verse in a monotonous tone. "Then I heard the voice of the Lord saying, whom shall I send? And who will go for us? And I said, Here am I. Send me!" Earl mentally kicked himself. He should have known better than to try to go toe to toe with his former professor. As he got up to leave, another verse came into mind, and he took a dig at Chris, even though he knew better. "So, you're going to blame this on God. I suppose you're going to pull out Romans 8:28 next: And we know that God causes everything to work together for the good of those who love God and are called according to his purpose for them."

Chris looked up, and in the same monotone voice that Earl had used in quoting Isaiah 6:8, Chris replied, "I don't have to. You just did."

How do you like that? He won't even give me the satisfaction of even acknowledging that I'm upset, thought Earl. Chris' next appointment showed up at the door, and Earl knew that it was to no avail to continue trying to change Chris' mind.

Earl checked out of the conference center hotel. Although the conference still had two days to go, Earl had had enough. He was in no mood to learn anything new, to reflect, or to do anything at the conference for that matter. Besides, if he had to be at Pinewood Church on Sunday, he needed to pack and let the church know that they were going to have another pastor in place almost immediately.

Earl started the car, and the radio came on. He had found a religious station that he had been listening to when he arrived at the conference center. The reception was not the greatest, and the radio crackled and popped and faded in and out. A radio preacher had a show on the radio at the moment. As Earl began to drive off the station cleared, and Earl could hear the twangy voice of the preacher.

"I've heard some good preachers in my day, but I wish I could have heard Jonah," declared the radio preacher. "Boy, he must have been some preacher. He was so good a preacher that God wanted him to go to Nineveh. But Jonah didn't want to go. In fact, he took a ship in the opposite direction. So, God sent a big fish to swallow Jonah and take him to Nineveh. When Jonah finally did preach, he convinced over one hundred and twenty thousand people to repent of their ways. We serve a God who gives second chances. Both Jonah and the people of Nineveh got a second chance."

Earl shook his head as he huffed through his nose. He punched the button, turning off the radio. "Ok, God. I get your point. I guess I'll go to Nineveh, in the guise of Pinewood."

Saturday morning after Thanksgiving, Earl was all packed. He had put the final suitcases in his car. It was amazing that all of his belongings could fit into several boxes and suitcases that could be contained within his car. He supposed that was one benefit of not having a family. If he didn't fear being accused of gambling, he would bet that at least one person would make a parting remark about him not having a family. Maybe he should remind them of what the apostle Paul said in First Corinthians about remaining unmarried. Several parishioners had come by to see Earl off, and they gathered around as he stood next to his car.

"The one good thing about not being married and having children is that I don't have very much to move." Earl tried to make it sound humorous, but no one laughed, not even Earl. He wondered why he made that remark since he didn't want others making it. He wanted to leave on a positive note; so, he quickly changed the subject. "I've loved the house here, and I hope it serves your new pastor well."

Ed Bowles stuck his head into the open car window. "We're going to miss you, Pastor. We all wish the bishop would have kept you here longer, but we can't be selfish. Best wishes." Earl backed out of the driveway and reluctantly headed off. As he looked back in the rearview mirror, he saw Elena Lopez waving bye.

Earl faced a five-hour drive on a gray day; the dreariness of the day pretty much reflected his inner feelings. If he were making the drive in late September or October, he would have had a colorful drive on the scenic backroads through more than one national forest. In November, the leaves had mostly already fallen, and only the evergreens provided some color. Earl drove without stopping, and he entered the outskirts of Pinewood in the early afternoon.

A shiver went through Earl from head to toe at the first glimpse of the church up ahead. The car weaved slightly as his arms spasmed from the shiver. Although about eleven years had passed since he had last seen the church, the landscape had changed somewhat, and the parking lot was full. He wondered what was going on at the church this time of the day on a Saturday. That's when Earl first noticed the sign. He should have noticed it sooner had he not been preoccupied with the dreadful thoughts of the place. The sign didn't read Pinewood Church. A huge sign read *Churchdale Barbeque*. Earl found an open parking spot. The building resembled the church he remembered. It had a steeple; it even had stained-glass windows that looked identical to the original ones. How could that be? Earl knew this was the building, but he double checked the address he had entered into his GPS.

Earl got out of the car and stretched his stiff limbs. A few people entered the building, and he observed some leaving, carrying boxes of what appeared to be take-out orders. Earl's stomach had been queasy from the trepidation of arriving at the church, but it now growled as the savory aroma of cooked pork, mixed with the outdoorsy scent of smoke from various hardwoods, wafted to his nose.

Nearby, a relatively new-looking housing development stood where he knew mobile homes had stood previously. "I know this is where the church was. Where is the mobile home park?"

Earl cautiously approached the entrance to the building. Several people passed by him commenting on how good the food was or saying that was the best barbeque they had ever eaten. A sign flashed *Open* as Earl wrapped his hand around the door handle. As he was about to pull, something inside of him stopped him. The hesitation turned into a pause, and then Earl released his hand completely. He turned his back to the church, or what was the church, and slinked toward the retreat of his car.

Although Earl had been tempted to go into the former church, now turned restaurant, something stopped his hand from pulling open the door. He didn't want to go inside; he couldn't go inside. Richard was right. In about one year's time, he ruined a church with a three-hundred-year-old history. In fact, *ruined* was too mild of a verb. He had caused this. He was the ruination, the destroyer, of the church. Jesus said, *And I tell you, you are Peter, and on this rock I will build my church, and the gates of hell shall not prevail against it.* Of course, Jesus was not talking about an individual church, but Earl felt that he was worse than the gates of hell. He could palpably feel Jesus' disappointment in him. That was why he could not go inside the former church that he had destroyed. This thought had always been a theme in his recurring nightmares. This was what he was afraid of. Now, reality confirmed his worse fears. This was Chris' fault for sending him here, Chris, his so-called friend. He had begged Chris not to send him here. Tears streamed down his cheeks and wet his shirt. He picked up his pace so that no one would see him as he hurried to the car. His nose had started to drip. When he was finally inside his car, he looked for tissue, but of course, he didn't have any. He wiped his eyes and nose with his shirt sleeve.

Earl sat in the car for a good fifteen minutes in order to compose himself. The tears had stopped quickly enough, but the pain lingered. He couldn't bear it here one day. How was he supposed to stay here for seven months? He prayed for the peace of Christ, but peace didn't come. Knowing nothing else to do, Earl drove toward town. The road going into town curved, with a smaller road cutting off to the side. Earl accidentally took the side road, realizing his mistake almost immediately. Rather than turning around, he decided to continue on. He could still get to town this way; it was just a little longer. The road used to pass by farmland, fields and woods. There were still some of each, but a mobile home development had gone up since he had been here last. He thought that the housing should look relatively new, but the mobile homes appeared old and worn out. Apparently, they had been brought in, perhaps relocated from the mobile home development that had been next to the old Pinewood Church. The whole area looked run down and poverty-stricken. Several teenagers were playing basketball on a court that was relatively new. At least something new had been put in, but the backboards were pretty shabby.

Eventually, Earl made it to the main road. He arrived in the town proper of Pinewood and parked in a two-hour free parking space. Pinewood looked very much the way it had a decade earlier. Some of the shops had changed, making way for new ones, but others were the same ones that had been in business for years. The population of the town was around twelve thousand people due to the expansive town limits, but it definitely had a small-town vibe. Several of the stores were putting up Christmas decorations. The bakery and the diner had traditional Christmas decorations. The hardware store had wooden toys from a bygone era when Santa Claus had a woodworking shop rather a technology and shipping hub. The old toys looked like antiques. Even the ornaments were vintage, circa 1940s. A massage business, calling itself *Massage on Main*, had the most unusual decorations. It had abstract art, both paintings and sculptures, that Earl could make neither heads nor tails of. One piece of art was primarily triangles of various colors, red, white, light peach, and green, that might have been Santa Claus. A metal sculpture might have been a reindeer. At the same time as the stores were decorating, the town crew was putting up the town's main street Christmas decorations. Earl chucked at the thought that these were the same ones he had seen before, and they looked like they had been purchased in the 1960s. He had to admit that he liked the street decorations and was glad that some things had not changed.

"Excuse me, sir." The voice boomed with authority, and Earl swung around to face a young man in his twenties. The man was tall with jet black hair. He wore kindness on his face the way some wore beards. He was dressed casually in jeans and a flannel shirt. "May I help you find something? You look a little lost?"

Earl started to reply that he had been here before but decided not to go into any details; so, he simply told the young man the most basic truth. "I'm trying to find Pinewood Church. I just came from where it was supposed to be, but there is a barbecue restaurant there."

A down-home smile cropped up on the young man's face. "I hope you went in and ate there. It's a very popular barbecue restaurant."

"No, I didn't eat there." The response came in bursts and pops like the sound of rifle reports. Although Earl wasn't really in the mood for conversation, he hoped the terseness of his response wasn't off-putting to someone who was merely trying to be helpful. Apparently, the young man had not taken it as off-putting.

"It's been featured nationally. I guarantee it will be some of the best barbecue you've ever eaten. They even have live music occasionally."

"I was just looking for Pinewood Church." There was the terseness again.

The man looked skyward, wrinkled his nose and audibly sniffed air through it as though the talk of barbecue had created an olfactory recollection of the aroma. "Well," he drawled, "Pinewood Church used to be there, but it moved from there close to ten years now. The new location is at the corner of First and Pine streets. The church bought the property from another church that closed. If you walk to the next block, you can see the church from there. I'd be happy to take you there."

"Thank you, but I have my car. Given your directions, I think I can find it easily enough."

Within two minutes, Earl was parked at the church parsonage, which was located on the same lot as the church, hearkening back to days gone by. The current Pinewood Church was probably about the same size as the former Pinewood Church. It was brick and didn't look as nice as the former church. The former church was as quaint as an old country church painting, complete with stained-glass windows, polished solid-oak pews, and creaking hardwood floors.

Seeing no welcoming committee, which he didn't really expect since he didn't tell anyone when he would arrive, Earl strode to the parsonage to inspect his temporary home. The first room he entered was large and open. No furniture was in the room; it was completely bare. "Great metaphor, God. I suppose this is the belly of the big fish that has spit me out on the doorsteps of the church, my own personal Nineveh. One of these days, I'm going to have to do a sermon on God's weird sense of humor." Earl's voice reverberated off the barren walls. "Great. Now I'm talking to myself. I wonder if Jonah did that in the belly of the big fish?" Several trips later, to and from the car, all of Earl's belongings sat on the floor in the parsonage. The rest of the rooms in the house were furnished. The furnishings were old and basic, but after the empty room he had seen upon entering the house, any furnishings were a welcome sight that he was thankful for.

Earl spent several hours putting away belongings. Fortunately, he had brought sheets and blankets; there were none in the parsonage. That was probably a good thing. He didn't know what the former pastor died of, and having his own sheets and blankets was a good idea.

Earl collapsed into bed that night. The old bed creaked with each turn, and the old parsonage played its own symphonic composition of sounds. His stomach growled, and he realized that he had not eaten anything that day. He had not brought any food, and if the town was like it used to be, there would be nothing open on Sunday morning to get for breakfast. Noon the next day would be the soonest he would be able to eat. He would have to make sure he gave a brief sermon.

Chapter Eight

Earl surveyed the Sunday morning worship service crowd. It definitely didn't fit the image in his visualization of him at a megachurch. Probably about one hundred people were in attendance, one-fifth the number of people who regularly attended his previous church. Believing this wasn't a demotion was difficult. His heart wasn't in the assignment. He had always worn his pulpit robe and stole with pride. Today, he wore a dress shirt, dress pants, and a jacket.

When the organist finished playing a hymn, Earl lumbered to the pulpit. A sea of blank expressions greeted him. He wasn't used to this. Congregants at his former church were always eager to see and hear him. Earl couldn't recall the last time he had been rattled before giving a sermon. He didn't really develop his talent for delivering sermons until after he left Pinewood the first time; so, the last time he was rattled was probably at Pinewood Church. He didn't want to use the word *cursed* when talking about a church, but he seemed to be anathema to this church. Earl offered a quick prayer that seemed to rebound off the ceiling in the sanctuary.

"Some of you may have been in the congregation when I first preached here in Pinewood around twelve years ago when the church was at its former location. I think I recognize a few faces." He tried to sound chipper, but the congregation was as quiet as a church mouse, as the saying went. He felt as though his stomach would rumble at any minute, and it would absolutely be heard by this crowd. "Since I've come back after all of these years, I thought an appropriate sermon would be the Prodigal Son." Earl smiled broadly, but still, the congregation remained silent and expressionless. "I think most of you know the story. A man returns home to his father and brother after being away for many years." Earl's brain seemed to go into a fog. All he could concentrate on was the reaction, or lack thereof, he was receiving from the congregation. "The father ... I mean the brother is not too happy to see him." Earl recalled back in seminary about an Old Testament comparison, which he decided to mention. "This is comparable to the story of Joseph and his brothers in the Book of Genesis. Both have themes of reconciliation." What was he doing? He was now just spouting theological connections without explaining the significance. He was supposed to be preaching, not teaching a theology class. What was the last thing he said? He couldn't remember. He had handwritten notes that he rarely needed to rely on, but he began visibly shuffling thorough them to see if something would spark his memory of where he was in the sermon. "The brother ... not Joseph's brother, but the Prodigal Son's brother ... didn't really like the fact that his brother came back home. Oh, I forgot to mention that the word prodigal means reckless and is usually an adjective." Really? Now, he was giving grammatical tips in his sermon! "Where was I? ... Oh ... The brother ... the older brother ... was faithful to his father and he thought his younger brother didn't appreciate his family. Jesus tells us that the father loved both sons, but he doesn't say what eventually happened with the two brothers' relationship." Earl fumbled through his notes once again and stole a quick glance at his watch.

Earl felt a gracious reprieve as people exited the church. He greeted them, but it was a blessing as each one left. When Earl saw the next person in line, he suddenly felt as though insects were gnawing his innards. It was the young man from yesterday who had given him directions to the new location of the church. Earl felt his face turning ten different shades of red, and he tried humor once more. "Well, I found the church." That was humor? "Thank you for the directions." Most of the people in the church would have probably been more thankful had the man given the wrong directions. Earl thought of saying that, but he was giving up attempting any more humor today.

"Glad to help," replied the man.

Another man, who appeared to be in his sixties, with gray and white hair held out his hand. "I remember you from when you first pastored our church. You were young and full of energy. As you can tell, we need some of that energy now."

"Yes. I would agree with you on that. Good to see you again after all these years."

"I'm Jerry Cloninger, by the way. We'll need to talk soon about the church's Christmas outreach activities. I'm on the committee. Christmas will be here in a few weeks."

After Jerry, a young woman, who appeared to be in her early thirties and a few years younger than himself, smiled. This was the first smile he had seen from a congregant. She seemed friendly. Then again, Ebenezer Scrooge would seem friendly in this crowd.

"Hello, Pastor. You probably don't remember me. My name is Harmony Waters. I was here the first time you were pastor at Pinewood Church."

"I don't believe that I do, but you would have been much younger." Harmony started at the comment; she was bug-eyed. Recognizing how his comment sounded, Earl quickly tried to placate her. "Not that you're not young now."

Harmony lowered her head slightly as she raised her eyebrows, "That was a quick recovery."

"I'm sorry. That didn't come out right." Harmony apparently ignored his attempted apology.

"Anyway, I had just finished college when you arrived, and I got an out-of-town job; so, I was mostly away, but I still saw you a good number of times when I visited my parents. I was really impressed with how you reached out to the community."

"Well, I wish I could have met your expectations today. This was probably the worst sermon I've ever preached, even compared to my first few."

Harmony's eyes beamed benevolence, and she lightly patted his hand. "I'm sure it must be very difficult to come back after all these years. Besides, action speaks louder than words." She nodded her head towards Jerry, who had already left. "I'm also on the Christmas Outreach Committee with Jerry. There are only a few of us, and Jerry and I are about the only two who do the work." Her eyes flashed a quizzical look. "Would you be able to meet tomorrow? We'll do all we can to get back on track. Remembering how you were from before, I'm sure we'll get back on track in no time."

Earl supposed that her comment about how he used to be was supplied as encouragement, but it struck the wrong chord. He quickly decided to take it for the compliment it was meant to be and answered accordingly. "Sure. I can use all the help I can get. How about lunch tomorrow?" Earl was surprised at how forward that sounded to his ears. He didn't mean it inappropriately. He also didn't know if her job would allow her the time. But it was too late to take back the comment now.

"That would be great. Do you want to meet at Churchdale Barbecue?"

Even the name, *Churchdale Barbecue*, sent alarm bells off in his head. "Uh ... Is there another place we could meet?"

"There's a diner on main street."

The tension, which he momentarily felt, washed away from his neck and shoulders. "Perfect. Around noon?"

A smile tinged her voice, if it were possible for a voice to smile. "That would be great. I have a flexible lunch hour. I'll see you then."

Earl's stomach was tied in knots. Although he hadn't eaten the day before, he didn't feel like eating now. In fact, he felt nauseated. Still, he supposed he needed to eat something. He ventured downtown to the diner. Of course, it was closed. There was a grocery store a couple of miles away, but he didn't feel like cooking.

Besides the stovetop and oven looked so dirty, it would probably erupt into flames if he tried cooking anything. Apparently, the former pastor must have eaten out a lot. Had Earl been at his former church, someone would have invited him for lunch. No one made that offer here.

The day had been long, and Earl was relieved when night approached, indicating that time was indeed passing that day, albeit slowly. The past two days had beaten Earl profusely. *Massage on Main*, had it been open, would have been well worth the money. He tried massaging his neck himself, but it was no help in removing the knots braiding his neck and shoulders. He grabbed his worn bible to read some passages that might help in releasing the knots when he heard three sharp raps against the old wooden parsonage door. He wondered who was here this time of night, and he slogged forward, carrying the tenseness in his body with him.

He opened the door, only to be greeted by darkness. He flipped the switch for the light hanging beside the door, but the dull glow of the four-hundred-fifty lumen bulb barely disturbed the darkness. No one was there, but he swore that he heard a knock on the door. He wasn't going to venture out. Turning his head from side to side was the only investigation he was going to undertake. Puzzled, he looked down. An envelope met his eyes, and he stooped, as though a board was tied to his back, to pick up the envelope. *Pastor Earl* was written on the envelope, and he took the envelope back inside so that the eight-hundred lumen bulb could provide more light. He was either going to have to invest in lightbulbs with more brightness or buy several lamps. The envelope wasn't sealed, and he pulled out the slip of paper inside. The print was produced by a printer, not handwritten. Only one sentence graced the paper, and it read, *You will receive three gifts before Christmas.* Earl's voice erupted in a chuckle restrained by exhaustion. "Only been here a couple of days and already getting pranked." Earl started to throw the paper away, but the waste basket was in another room; so, instead, he plopped it onto a table.

It wasn't extremely late, but Earl didn't feel like looking at tv, reading, or anything. He went to bed, but his stomach growled and gnawed at him. He was hungry, but there was still no food in the parsonage. He got up, found cleaning products, and began working on cleaning the stovetop and oven. It ate up a few hours, and afterwards, he felt as though he could finally go to sleep. At least the stovetop and oven were clean now. He'd stock up on some food tomorrow so that he wouldn't be in a situation again with no food.

Chapter Nine

Earl detected the slight odor of residual grease from breakfast as he sat at a table waiting for Harmony. Although Earl saw the Christmas decorations the other day as they were being put up, he saw them from the outside. Inside, he could see there were severalfold the number he thought had been put up. All of the tables had Christmas table runners across the middle of the tables, which had to be a huge daily cleaning expense with the down-home country cooking of the diner, what with the gravies, condiments for burgers, and waitress-poured coffee and tea. A snow globe was placed near the register that people apparently shook for wishes. Santa chalkboards displayed the daily specials, and strands of Christmas lights that would have stretched three football fields lined the walls and ceilings. All sorts of Christmas Nick Nacks cluttered the restaurant as if the owner had bought out an entire Christmas Store.

The door opened, and once again Earl heard part of a Christmas Song played for the umpteenth time in the short amount of time he had been there. Harmony pranced to the music as she gracefully made her way over to Earl. She smiled a smile that would melt the stingiest heart as she took her place at the table in a seat across from Earl. He couldn't help but return the smile, even if it was a toned-down version of Harmony's smile.

Earl had been studying the menu, but he noticed that Harmony had not bothered to pick one up. Intrigued, he asked, "What's good here?"

Without hesitation, Harmony rattled off, "I usually get a Chef Salad with Vinaigrette dressing on the side and water." The waitress seemingly appeared out of thin air, but then again, she wore Christmas clothes, which allowed her to blend in seamlessly with her surroundings. She wrote down Harmony's order. Earl had been looking at something not as heart-friendly but decided to match Harmony's order. "I'll have the same," he replied while thinking somewhat begrudgingly of the missed opportunity as he ordered. The waitress made a single mark on the ticket, duplicating Harmony's order. In the blink of any eye, the camouflaged waitress disappeared into the sea of Christmas decorations.

"I hope you don't mind that I ordered the salad. I didn't want our new pastor saying something along the lines of *You're not overly slim*." An infectious laugh burst forth from Harmony. "I'm kidding. That is my usual order, but I wanted to have a little fun at your expense."

A sly smile, like that of a child getting caught with two handfuls of cookies when he was allowed only one, etched its way onto Earl's face. "I suppose I deserved that." Earl wasn't sure what to say next. He rarely spent much time alone with someone of the opposite gender. What he ended up saying was rather bland, and he realized how out of practice he was in such a situation. "Before we start talking about the church's Christmas outreach, tell me a little about yourself, if you don't mind. I like to get to know the congregation." Earl sensed that Harmony had not quite had her satisfaction of playful banter, but she grew serious as she contemplated his request.

"I don't mind," she answered sweetly but resignedly. "After college, I got a job as a bank auditor. If this were a date, now would be the time when my date would make some excuse to leave. It's not a very exciting career, and it must give some insight regarding my personality that turns men off."

Earl was intrigued by her response, and he leaned in as if sharing a secret. "I think you have a great personality."

Harmony's eyes sparkled as they grew wide, and she feigned exasperation in her mannerisms and speech. "So, I'm not old, and I have a great personality. You really know how to make a woman feel appreciated."

Earl was right, she wasn't ready to let go just yet of playful banter. "I'm sorry. I guess I'm not making a very good first impression. Or second impression, actually." Earl wished he had said something wittier.

Harmony apparently resigned herself to the fact the Earl was not in as playful of a mood as she was. "To continue answering your question, when I got the job as a bank auditor, I traveled a lot for several years. Then, I was an associate vice president at corporate headquarters. I came back to Pinewood about a year ago when my father suffered a heart attack." A look of realization seemed to show on her face that her parents were getting older. "I wanted to help him and my mother during that time. The bank allowed me to have the job as the local branch manager at the bank in town. My father is doing much better now, and I'd like to eventually go back to corporate headquarters."

"I hope you'll at least wait until after Christmas before you move away."

Harmony smiled flirtatiously. Apparently, he let his true feelings show that he would like to see her around a lot more. That feeling changed when Harmony answered. Apparently, he was a hard read.

"Don't worry. I'll help you with our Christmas Outreach. You know ... when I traveled, I never could belong to a church; so, I would go to different churches in the cities I was in. I saw you preach a few times at some of your churches. I was always inspired when I heard your sermons. They were among the best I ever heard."

Earl sighed audibly at the thought of yesterday's sermon. "Well, yesterday must have been terribly disappointing. I've never preached so poorly in my life." He didn't want to sound as though he were the sole member of his own pity party; so, he quickly redirected. "Why didn't you tell me who you were when you visited the other churches?"

Harmony focused her attention on the ceiling, looking pensive as she prepared a response. "I doubt you would have remembered me. In my experience, telling something like that always comes off as awkward."

Earl was about to say that he wished she had told him, but his thoughts were interrupted by the waitress bringing their food. Earl stole an admiring glance at the woman sitting before him, and he could read Harmony's thoughts that showed plainly on her face. She was trying to carry the conversation that he was regrettably forfeiting.

"So, knowing how you were when you were here before, I'm sure you're really great with community outreach now."

Earl knew the expression on his face had betrayed him. Thoughts of his recurring nightmare and his horrific episode at Churchdale Barbeque flooded his being, biting into his soul. He lost his composure at his sense of inadequacy. Suddenly, he was back at his previous church, dodging all attempts of any community outreach, supplying all sorts of excuses to Zola, Carl, Reverend Jung, and numerous others. He just couldn't get past this issue, which was why he wanted to focus solely on delivering sermons. He felt like a cad as he heard the words come out of his mouth. "Wow, I just remembered that I have another appointment I need to get to. I completely forgot about it. I'm so sorry. I truly apologize for my forgetfulness. Will Wednesday night work for you? I'll call and see if Jerry can make it then. We can meet at the church." Earl blurted out the sentences like a rapid-fire machine gun. Regret gnawed at him over the complete manufacturing of such an excuse; it was an outright lie.

A quick glance at Harmony gave Earl the impression she had just witnessed aliens walking into the restaurant. Her eyes were about to pop out of their sockets with her eyebrows rising toward her hairline, and her mouth was as wide open as the singing fish on the wall that was singing Jingle Bells. "But you didn't even touch your food."

"Sorry. Gotta run." Earl slapped down money on the table to cover both of their meals. In the entire time he had been in Pinewood, he had yet to eat anything.

"Yes ... Wednesday night will be fine. Hey! Do you want this boxed to go?" he heard her say over the singing fish. The cold slap of air in his face as he pushed open the door felt good against his clammy skin. Once outside, he felt safe in this sanctuary, a temporary reprieve from his own personal hell.

Chapter Ten

As Earl slept, his eyes began to move rapidly. His heart raced, and he breathed in quick shallow breaths.

A younger Earl stood outside of the old Pinewood Church. Broken shards of stained glass lay at his feet. He surveyed the damage; several of the priceless windows were broken beyond repair. A barefoot boy in ragged clothes stood near Earl, looking at the destruction, with a rock in his dirt-stained hand. Richard had driven by mere minutes after the vandalism. Earl arrived less than one minute before Richard did. Earl had led a bingo night for the seniors in the mobile home development. Richard stomped around the church inspecting the damage. He glared at Earl as he stormed over to him. His anger seemed to be growing by the second. The veins in Richard's neck were pulsing rivers of fury, and the anger poured from his mouth as he launched into a bitter diatribe.

"This is what happens when you involve outsiders who have no intention of supporting the church." Richard angrily pointed a finger in the direction of the mobile homes. "Those people you've been trying to help in the trailer park are beyond help," insinuated Richard as he stomped the ground. Richard's eyes bore into Earl's, and he spoke slowly, loudly, and deliberately, "All you've done is invite bad elements into our church. No good deed goes unpunished." When Richard finished yelling, he was so mad that he spat on Earl's shoes.

Panic and dread showed on Earl's face. "I can make this right."

Richard's nose winced as though he smelled pungent cow manure. When he spoke, his voice was eerily calm and hateful and the same time. "The only decent thing you can do is leave."

"I'm sorry," was all Earl could squeak out.

Richard's voice changed once more. It was a pleading voice, one on the verge of tears, one like that of a father who had lost his son to death and couldn't understand how the doctor could not have saved him. "You were supposed to help the people in our church. That boy from the trailer park has a rock in his hand. What other evidence do you need? The only thing you've accomplished is to drive a wedge in the church. We deserved a shepherd for our church, not a wanna be social worker who let wolves in amongst the sheep."

In an instant, Earl was now standing in the church boardroom, like an accused defendant, in front of a group of Church Council Leaders. The seven-member group of church leaders were all older stern-faced men. The head lay leader and self-appointed guardian of the church's legacy, Richard Coldwell, had just reminded the other councilmen that he was a descendant of one of the founding families of the church. Richard was angry to the point of being hysterical. He looked as though he were Satan accusing humankind, red-faced and scowling with an outstretched arm and pointed finger. His words were harsh and biting, penetrating the toughest armor into the very core of a person. Earl quivered at his presence.

"In one year," accused Richard, spittle spewing out of his mouth as he pointed and glared at Earl, "you've ruined a church that has almost a three-hundred-year-old history. We've called the bishop and asked him to appoint another pastor. We demand your resignation immediately. I swear if it's the last thing I do, I'll make sure you never serve another church again."

The other members of the Church Council, all still stern-faced, nodded their heads in agreement.

Earl's body was tense, almost paralyzed, as he awoke from the vivid nightmare. His breathing was shallow, and his heart raced. His night clothes were soaked with a cool sweat. Sometimes, he would have bits and pieces of the nightmare. Tonight, he experienced the full episode. Pinewood wasn't helping him to overcome his demons. It was making them worse.

Earl looked at the clock on the nightstand beside the bed. It showed two o'clock in the morning. He knew he couldn't go immediately back to sleep. Reaching over to the nightstand he stretched and struggled to turn on the lamp. Feeling antsy, he sat up in bed, causing it to creak loudly in protest. He pulled open the top drawer of the nightstand, expecting to find a bible. Inside, though, were several church directories over the years. He searched for one of his time at the church, found it, and pulled it out. Opening it up, he saw a picture of himself as pastor of the church. He flipped to the back and saw a picture of Harmony Waters and her parents. Harmony said she had just finished college when he arrived. The picture showed a pretty, young woman who looked to be in her early twenties. "Not old and you have a nice personality. Why didn't I add beautiful to that?" Earl flipped back to the front of the book and saw a full-page picture of the lead layperson, Richard Coldwell. Earl shuddered, closed the directory, and tossed it back into the nightstand.

Earl closed his eyes and prayed, "Lord, I don't want to be here. I know your purpose in bringing me here, but I don't have the confidence or the ability anymore to do what you want. Please give me the strength to bear this."

Chapter Eleven

Although the call for the Wednesday night meeting had been put out to the entire Christmas Outreach Ministry Committee, only Harmony and Jerry, as previously predicted, actually showed up to meet with Earl. The embarrassment that Earl faced when he left Harmony stranded at the diner helped to serve a positive purpose. Earl wanted to make up for fleeing the scene, and if he was ever going to conquer his fear of failing the church because of his outreach ability, he needed to do it now or never. Those two things motivated him either to succeed at outreach or fail on a grand scale.

"So, what does the church typically do as part of the Christmas Outreach Ministry?" asked Earl.

Jerry spoke, as though he had given the same answer to the same question for years. "We usually have a toy drive. I'm friends with Farmer Brown. He's usually supplied Christmas trees at a very reasonable price for us to resell to make money for the toy drive."

Earl wondered how acting as a middleman in selling Christmas Trees would raise much money, but if this is what the church did every year, who was he to argue? His main concern was being able to sell enough trees in the amount of time they had left. Some people put up trees the weekend after Thanksgiving. It was now December, and they certainly wouldn't start selling trees tomorrow. "It's a little late to start, but I think we can still pull it off."

Harmony's body became alert at the comment, as if Earl had thrown down the gauntlet. "I think we can do more than that."

Jerry stroked the stubble on his chin as he thought. "We have a small congregation. If the pastor thinks we got a late start, maybe we should forego the outreach ministry this year. It's only been a few weeks since our former pastor passed away, and Earl is only here temporarily. I think we need time to heal and regroup."

"What better way to heal than to help those in need?" responded Harmony.

Watching Jerry and Harmony go at it was like watching two political candidates with opposing views.

"What do you think, Pastor?" asked Harmony.

Earl desperately wanted to cancel. He had the perfect excuse, and he had even been perfectly set up to deliver the excuse. But he had decided he was going to do his best to succeed this time, and to do that he had to make an attempt. "Canceling would be the sensible thing to do, ... but I was sent here specifically for the purpose of doing outreach. The Christmas Tree idea sounds good to me."

Harmony rushed in to comment. "If we have enough money, we could use some to buy food in addition to toys. The town still has a very poor area that desperately needs food this time of year. We also need to do more for the children than just give them toys. They need to feel appreciated in other ways. Maybe we could do a hayride for the children and a Christmas movie night."

Earl was impressed by Harmony. She was *go big or go home.* Maybe that was the reason only two people regularly attended the committee meeting; they were intimidated at the scale of the ideas, or they lacked the necessary amount of time to commit to them.

"I'm sure Farmer Brown would be willing to help with the hayride," added Jerry. "I don't think we'll get much help from the congregation, but I'm willing to try. I'm retired; so, I have the time. You'll need to get approval from the Church Council though. Maybe we can see what Victorious Life Church is doing. We don't need to duplicate or have things on the same night."

Jerry seemed pretty easy-going. He also seemed to go with the wind. He easily vacillated between doing nothing and stepping up the game a notch.

"Pastor, can you handle both of those?" asked Jerry.

Earl nodded reluctantly. He didn't recall a church by the name of Victorious Life from his previous stint as pastor. "What is Victorious Life Church, and why are we specifically checking with them and not any other churches?"

Harmony rushed to answer the question. "Victorious Life Church is a relatively new church in town. It's probably the biggest church in town as well. They tend to do a lot of activities that draw in a lot of people. We don't want to compete with them by having activities on the same day. Most people would more than likely go to the events hosted by Victorious Life Church."

"That includes members of our own church," added Jerry. "It would be really embarrassing for us to hold an event at the same time and our congregation go to theirs instead of ours."

"Gotcha," replied Earl.

On Thursday night, Earl stood before the seven-member Church Council. At least this was a different building and a different church council than he faced previously at Pinewood Church. This council was not as old or stern looking as the one he faced before. And they were not all men. And Richard Coldwell was no longer a member of the church, much less the council. Although the council was more diverse, the lead layperson was still an older male and probably the most stern-faced of the group. The council didn't typically meet on Thursday evenings, but Earl requested a special meeting since time was important in accomplishing the fund-raising goal.

Ted Long, the lead layperson, was in his sixties. His last name adequately described his height, which was six feet two inches. His hair was thin, and although it had lost some of its darkness, it was still relatively dark for his age. "The council has voted to approve the Christmas Outreach activities you proposed," reported Ted. "Be careful though, Pastor. Too few trees won't bring in enough money. Too many trees will cost us more than we'll make. We want you to regularly keep us informed."

Earl nodded and was thankful for them to see his back.

The next morning, Earl set out on his second task of seeing what Victorious Life Church was doing so as not to duplicate activities. Victorious Life Church was outside of the town limits. It was a larger church than Pinewood, both in physical size and in membership. Victorious Life Church had not been in existence when Earl was previously in Pinewood. When he arrived at the church, he was floored that such a new and modern-looking church existed in the town.

Earl chatted with the church secretary as he waited outside of the pastor's study. She appeared to be in her forties and was very professional and organized. From her dress and appearance, Earl guessed she was fairly well-to-do financially. Her speech was elegant and clipped, and there was nothing stray on her desk. He imagined she was as good at her job as Zola was, only in a different way. The woman's phone beeped, and without looking down, she indicated that the pastor would see him. Earl thanked her for her hospitality and crossed the short distance to the pastor's study in a few steps.

Earl stopped within three steps of entering the study, and he felt his jaw drop. "You!" The greeting didn't sound very professional as Earl blurted it out, but he was taken by surprise. Standing up to greet him was the young man he met in town who had given him directions and who showed up at his Sunday morning service.

"Me," beamed the man.

Earl was still somewhat dumbfounded as he watched the young man cheerfully stride over to him and offer a hearty handshake.

"I'm Pastor William Lorie."

Earl shook off the silly look on his face. "Why didn't you identify yourself the other day when we met?"

"Why didn't you identify yourself?" mirrored William.

Earl shrugged as he replied, "Touché." Earl knitted his eyebrows together has he contemplated something. "You were in the congregation on Sunday morning. Did you not have to preach then yourself?"

"Our services are earlier." William puffed out his chest. "And I wanted to see the famous Pastor Earl Stanley. I've read you're one of the up-and-coming pastors in America."

Earl could feel the heat from his reddened face as he recalled his flop of a sermon. "I've been apologizing about my sermon to everyone who was there. I might as well apologize to you too."

A corner of William's mouth rose as he apparently brushed off Earl's apology with a swat of his hand. "No need to apologize. It took a lot of courage to preach your first sermon in this town after all of the years since you've been gone. I don't know that I could have done it myself."

"I see you've heard about my infamous past here," deadpanned Earl.

A look of confusion crept onto William's face. "I've heard about the good you did while you were here."

Earl sighed in resignation. "That's what people keep telling me."

William's eyebrows formed perfect arches over his eyes, as if he still didn't understand what Earl seemed to find as a problem. "Well, they can't all be wrong. Now, what can I do for you?" William paused, and a smile suddenly appeared on his face, "Do you need some more directions?"

Earl found himself laughing at the comment. This was probably the first time he had laughed since his return to Pinewood. "Not the driving kind. With all that's happened recently at Pinewood Church, we're getting a late start on what the church typically does at Christmas. Our committee thought it might be a good idea to see what you were doing, so that we won't be competing with each other."

William appeared to be taking in all that Earl was saying, but his response seemed to indicate otherwise. "Let me show you our sanctuary, and we can talk."

As the two pastors entered the sanctuary of Victorious Life Church, Earl had to admit he was impressed. If he preached in a sanctuary as beautiful and as modern as this one, he would want to show it off as well to anyone who came by. The minimalist design created a look of openness, which in turn allowed the sanctuary to emanate a sense of tranquility that Earl could feel flow through him. The sanctuary contained no pews. Instead, lightweight, stackable, ergonomic chairs with back and seat cushions formed a semi-circular layout. This allowed the space to be multi-functional. The polished wood flooring reflected the incoming sunlight as it passed through large windows to provide a warm atmosphere. The walls were painted in a warm neutral tone, and a few strategically placed banners featured select scripture verses and even a few secular inspirational quotes. The pulpit was a sleek-looking fixture of glass and metal that rested on a slightly elevated stage. Behind the pulpit, a beautiful stained-glass window was located high on the wall.

Earl could not stop looking all around the sanctuary. "You have a beautiful church here, and the stained glass is exquisite."

"Thanks. I love stained glass, but these days, it's difficult to adorn an entire church; so, we settled with one to create a focal point."

"It's definitely that, and this is a large church."

"We started this church a few years ago, and God has really blessed us."

Earl could think of nothing else to say other than, "He certainly has." Earl continued admiring the sanctuary and feeling the sense of peace it provided. "Does this church belong to a particular denomination?"

"We're a non-denominational Christian church. Our mission is to bring people to God, not divide them into categories."

"I'm impressed."

Apparently, William had accomplished his purpose of showing Earl the sanctuary, and he began to answer the question that Earl had asked earlier. "So, you want to know what we're doing for Christmas." William paused as Earl refocused his attention on the reason he came to this church in the first place. "We have an angel tree, a food drive, a candlelight walk downtown, and a Christmas carnival for children and youth. It's not going to be very big, just something to allow them to have a little fun." William grabbed a flyer from the pulpit and handed it to Earl. "Here's a schedule if you want to plan around our activities."

Earl reviewed the events listed on the flyer. "We were going to do a toy drive and perhaps a food drive as well. Maybe we should not do those since your church is doing them."

William shook his head slightly. "I hope you keep those activities. We have a large poor population in town. All it did was move from its location beside Churchdale Barbeque to another location. There are so many needy families that collecting more toys and food would be a great help. When you decide what you're doing, I would appreciate it if you could give us your schedule. We'd love to help promote it."

"Certainly. Thank you for your time, and it was great to meet you in your official capacity."

"It's good to see you as well. Keep in touch."

As Earl trekked back to his car, he thought about his meeting with William. He really liked the young man. He had a slightly mischievous side, keeping secret the fact that he was a pastor, but Earl couldn't think of enough good qualities to describe him … genuine, caring, kind, helpful, modest, unpretentious, charismatic, smart, and the list went on.

The next night, Harmony, Jerry, and Earl met at Pinewood Church to discuss the church's Christmas Outreach Ministry. Once again, they were the only three who were present. "Here are copies of the activities that Victorious Life Church has planned," stated Earl as he handed copies of the flyer to Harmony and Jerry. "There's more on here than what Pastor Lorie mentioned to me."

Harmony took a moment to scan the list of scheduled activities before replying, "There's a lot here. Of course, they are a larger church, but we can still keep what we've planned. And there are definitely gaps between the events where we can do ours."

Had Earl not known Harmony's occupation, he would have guessed some career close to her actual one. The confident assertiveness and her organizational and observational skills all pointed to a smart, efficient, and dedicated woman. Earl found himself staring at Harmony. He realized he was staring and diverted his gaze. Harmony had apparently not noticed his staring, and he hoped Jerry hadn't. Maybe it was a good thing no one else was there, else someone would have noticed.

The sound of Jerry's voice interrupted his thoughts as Jerry volunteered the information he had found. "I have some news regarding Farmer Brown. He'll provide the trees at an extremely low price. He'll cut them; we just have to pick them up. We can also do the hayride at his farm. He'll let us use some of his wagons and horses, and we can set up a hot chocolate stand and show a movie in an area he uses for venues. We'll just have to bus people out there."

Harmony blew an exasperated breath from her mouth. "That's going to be difficult."

This was the first time that Earl had heard Harmony voice anything other than pure, unadulterated optimism.

She continued her thought. "Most people can probably get to the church, but it would be nice to have a pickup area at the mobile home neighborhood for those who can't get to the church."

"Good idea," replied Earl. "We'll just have to find transportation. We don't have a church bus."

"Maybe you can ask Pastor William for some help," declared Harmony in a casual manner. "Victorious Life Church has a couple of buses."

Now it was Earl's turn to blow an exasperated breath. "I can, but I hate to impose on them. They already have numerous events they're doing. This feels like it will be adding a burden on them."

"The worst he can say is no," offered Harmony.

Earl wondered why people always said that expression. It was never that simple. First, it was a matter of politeness. You could ask for anything from anybody if you thought that the worst they could say was *no*. Second, it set the asker up to be embarrassed. Third, it set up the person being asked to feel embarrassed or obligated, or pressured, etc. He would expect that mindset from a salesperson or a telemarketer, whose goal was to make a sale or prove a point at any means necessary, but it just didn't seem like an effective or appropriate strategy for usage. And why should they rely on another church to do the work their own church wouldn't do? "This is all pretty ambitious if you don't think we'll get much help from our own congregation."

Harmony lifted her chin, giving her face a chiseled look of confidence. "We can pull it off. I've printed up some flyers advertising the Christmas Tree sale. We can go tomorrow to see if the stores will let us post them, and then we need to get a Christmas wish list from the children so that we know what toys to buy."

Jerry fell back in his chair and let out a huge breath. "I have two doctor's appointments tomorrow. I won't be able to help tomorrow."

Earl had to stifle a laugh. Poor Jerry. He was a hard worker, but Jerry looked relieved to have appointments that allowed him to get out of the work tomorrow. Harmony was a tough cookie. He supposed she had to be to have been as successful as she was in the banking jobs she had.

"That's ok. The pastor and I can work together."

"Are you able to take the time away from your job to help?" quizzed Earl.

"I have some vacation days built up I can take, and the Assistant Bank Manager can handle the bank. Besides, she owes me several favors."

Earl appreciated the help, and maybe he could make up for walking out on her the other day. He had to admit he was attracted to her. She seemed to be at least slightly attracted to him, unless her personality just naturally came across as a little flirtatious. Earl had never been married. He had never come close to marriage. Sometimes, he longed to have a family, but he wanted the right person. He had just never met the right person. Was Harmony the right person? Perhaps. He didn't think Harmony had ever been married either. She was pretty and would have had to have drawn the attention of many. She was a little bossy though, which could be off-putting to a lot of men. Actually, her strong confidence was more than likely mistaken for bossiness. Maybe he was attracted to her because of her confidence. It was certainly of great help to him. If he ever had any self-confidence, it was abashed years ago. He just needed to be cautious not to let her become a crutch for him, accomplishing what he needed to accomplish. And if he liked her, he needed to like her for herself, not for what she could do to help him.

Earl had literally just finished the meeting with Jerry and Harmony when his phone rang. He took it out of his pocket and saw that Bishop Christian Goodpaster was calling. This should be interesting, Earl thought. He wondered if Chris was just checking up on him or if he was feeling guilty for sending him to Pinewood. Only one way to find out. Earl answered the phone. "Hello, Chirs. I hope this isn't a pocket dial!"

"No, not at all," came Chris' voice over the phone. "I was just calling to see how you were doing and to make sure you got settled in ok."

"Why didn't you tell me the church had moved locations?"

"I suppose I just assumed you would put the address into your GPS. Besides, you didn't give me much of a chance."

"I suppose that's true. Well, I won't lie to you. It's not been easy, but I haven't been runoff yet either. Trying to pull off the Christmas outreach ministry they usually do has been challenging."

"It would be challenging for anyone, but I have confidence in you. I mainly called to make sure there were no hard feelings. Let's try to meet early in the new year. I'll buy you dinner."

"No hard feelings. I know you were doing what God called you to do. I never thought about how tough of a job you have with church assignments. I appreciate that you called. Thanks for checking up on me."

"Merry Christmas, Earl."

"Merry Christmas, Chris."

Earl disconnected from the call. It was nice of Chris to check on him. He had been tough on Chris, but he was glad to have Chris as a friend, and he didn't want to jeopardize that.

The next morning, Earl met Harmony outside of the diner. The morning was cold, and a few people hurried along the sidewalk, their breaths forming expanding clouds. As one of the breath clouds dissipated, Earl saw another one. This one belonged to Harmony as she gracefully paraded toward him. She looked nice in her winter ensemble: a navy peacoat over a black turtleneck, white culottes, and black suede pumps. Cheek dimples greeted Earl as she smiled. "Good morning, Pastor. Are you ready?"

"Only if you'll start calling me Earl rather than pastor."

"Are you ready, Earl?" Most everything she said to him seemed flirtatious. He didn't know if she was just that way with him; he certainly hoped so.

"I'm ready," answered Earl with equal flirtatiousness, causing Harmony to do a double take and to broaden her smile. "Where do you want to go first?" he asked.

"Since we're here at the Mainstreet Diner, let's try here first."

The diner was almost steamy compared to outside. The smell of bacon and coffee scented the air. Only two or three tables were open, and a sign read, *Seat Yourself.* Multiple indistinguishable conversations crisscrossed the space. Apparently, the coffee here was strong to inspire this much energy this early in the morning. Unfortunately, the singing fish still sung every time someone opened the door. Would this fish ever annoy one person too many? As busy as the diner was, Earl wondered why anyone took the time to turn it on.

"Good morning, Harmony," called out the lightly accented voice of a woman who appeared to be in her forties. The woman wiped her forearm across her brow and looked as though she could have used some of the outside cold air to cool off.

"Good morning, Samantha. Looks like you've got a crowd this morning."

"We do. Nothing brings out an appetite like cold weather. And unfortunately, we're down a waitress and a cook. It's the flu season, you know. So, I'm doing triple duty this morning." Samantha wiped her brow with her forearm once more and seemed to notice that Harmony wasn't seating herself according to the sign. "My next loan payment is not due until next week. I didn't know the bank manager was personally coming by to collect it!" joked Samantha.

Harmony waved off the words with a flip of her hand and made a "pfft" sound. "No, I'm not here for your loan payment. I'd like to introduce you to Earl Stanley, pastor of Pinewood Church. Earl, this is Samantha Estes, owner of the diner."

Samantha eyed Earl, up and down, sizing him up before speaking. He must have passed the test. "Nice to meet you, Earl. Well, I'm pleased to see that Harmony finally has a boyfriend!"

Earl stole a quick gaze at Harmony to catch her blushing. It was a look that seemed uncharacteristic for her. The blush quickly faded, and had Earl not been quick in looking, he would have missed it.

"Oh ... Earl isn't my boyfriend ..."

Even though the blush was gone from Harmony's face, the slight stutter conveyed her fluster.

"It's a pleasure to meet you, Samantha."

"We just wanted to see if we could post a flyer advertising the Christmas Tree sale our church is doing," chimed Harmony.

"Can I skip this month's loan payment if I say *yes?*"

"Sorry, but the bank wouldn't let me be the manager much longer if I did that," replied Harmony dryly.

Samantha placed her fists on her hips. "I'm kidding. Of course, you can put up a flyer."

Earl handed Samantha a flyer, and she posted it near the register.

"Thank you and have a blessed day," added Earl as he and Harmony turned to leave the diner and to brace themselves to head back out into the cold.

"You know." Samantha's voice stopped them, and they turned back to face her. Samantha appeared to be in deep thought as she looked off to the side to some insignificant spot on the wall. "This time of year, the town has a lot of people with food insecurities. If you ever plan to have an actual meal around Christmas for those in need, let me know. I would be glad to help cook some food and take it wherever you need it. Everyone needs a good, hot, Christmas meal. I'm sure some of the other eateries would help also."

"That's a wonderful idea," acknowledged Earl. "We'll let you know."

Earl held the door open for Harmony. The cold air caused her to immediately shiver even before she was outside. She leaned against Earl, and he could feel the subtle shivers flutter through her body. He ran his hands across her shoulders and down the lengths of her arms. He doubted she could feel any sensation of touch through the peacoat, but he felt a stronger shutter when he touched her. Harmony looked up and into Earl's eyes, and he sensed an unspoken thank you pass from her eyes to his.

Earl and Harmony spent the rest of the morning visiting various businesses: the hardware store, bookstore, florist, general store, massage studio, beauty shop, bakery, antique store, clothing store, and more. Everyone let them post flyers.

They distributed all of their flyers and ended up back at the diner shortly before lunch and just in time to see Pastor William Lorie as he was about to enter the diner for lunch. William was his jovial self and gave them both a friendly wave as he came over to speak.

"How is everything going?" asked William. "I see you've put up flyers around town."

"Yes," answered Earl. "Now we need to get a wish list of presents for children."

"We got our list from the local social services agency, but we haven't been back in a couple of weeks. I imagine more names have come in since then."

"We'll head there next and pay them a visit."

William headed for the diner but stopped short of opening the door. He turned around and called out, "Hey, tomorrow night is our candlelight walk through the town. Why don't you and Harmony come along?"

"I'd love to, if Harmony can."

"Definitely!"

William turned to enter the diner, but this time it was Earl who stopped him from entering. "Oh, before I forget. Here's our schedule of Christmas activities. We've worked around your dates. For the hayride, we're going to have to transport people to Mr. Brown's farm. Only a few people in our congregation have an SUV or minivan. I wondered if you could help us with the transportation."

"Certainly! We have a couple of small buses. I also have a friend in a nearby town with a bus tour company. I'm sure I can convince him to loan one of his bigger buses and a driver free of charge for the night."

"That's wonderful. I just don't want to create an added burden for you since this wasn't one of your activities."

"Nonsense. The more Christmas spirit we can spread, the better. I also have a favor to ask of you, but in no way should you feel obligated."

The statement reminded Earl of what Harmony had said previously. *The worst he can say is no.* After William's gracious help, how could he now say *no*?

"How about meeting me tomorrow morning around eight a.m. for breakfast here at the Mainstreet Diner if you can? I'll buy."

"I'd be glad to." That was easy enough.

Earl thought about asking Harmony if she wanted to eat lunch at the diner when she pulled a power bar from her purse.

"I was just going to ask you if you wanted to eat lunch here."

Harmony handed him the power bar, winked at him, and pulled another one from her purse. Her eyes gleamed mischievously, and she showed her pearly whites. "We don't need you suddenly remembering you have another commitment and leaving an entire plate of food untouched."

Harmony seemed good-natured about the lunch incident from the other day. He hoped that truly was the case. Earl begrudgingly ate his bland-tasting power bar. He supposed it served him right for abandoning and wasting good food. So far, from the meals he had in this town, or lack of meals as was more accurate the case, he wasn't going to gain any weight.

After their so-called lunch, Earl and Harmony visited the local social services agency. The representative there told them that they had given numerous wishes to Victorious Life Church, but they'd had lots of additional ones since then. The representative gave them a decent-sized list that was more than Earl expected. The church was going to have to sell a lot of trees to raise enough money to meet the needs of these families.

"We've done a lot in one day," suggested Earl. "Maybe we'll pull this off after all."

"We will. You'll see."

Chapter Twelve

The next morning, Earl arrived early at the diner for breakfast, only to find William already sitting at a table. Earl wended his way through the maze of tables and joined William. "I'm early. How long have you been here?"

"Not long."

Earl noticed that William had a devotional study booklet on the table, and he had apparently been reading and reflecting on the daily lesson. "How are you able to do a devotional in all of this hubbub?"

William rested his arms and hands on the table. "I've generally found that God calls me to act in chaotic situations. It dawned on me on day, or maybe I received divine inspiration, that my devotional study needed to be in a similar environment."

Earl raised his head, and his eyes automatically diverted to a corner of the ceiling as he contemplated what William had just told him. "Well, that certainly sounds logical. To each his own, I guess. I'm used to peace and quiet for devotion and reflection though. I don't know if I could do what you do and have anything stick with me."

"As you said, to each his or her own. But give it a try sometime. I have to admit that it does take a little getting used to, but you may find it works fine for you."

A harried looking waitress with her hair tied in a ponytail scurried over to their table. Apparently, the diner was still short-staffed today. Earl didn't see Samantha, but she may have been in the kitchen cooking. The waitress pulled a notepad from a pocket in her waist apron and drew the pen that was tucked behind her ear the way a swashbuckler would draw a sword from its sheath. "Are you ready to order?" She spoke in a monotone voice and didn't look up from her notepad. This woman meant business. Earl could tell she was a hard worker who could multitask with the best of them.

"I'll just have a cup of coffee," ordered Earl.

"Hold on," urged William. "When I said I would buy, I meant more than a cup of coffee. Don't hurt my feelings. Order some food. The western omelet is really good here."

Earl hadn't had a decent meal since he'd been in Pinewood, and an omelet sounded really good. In fact, just the thought of it started his mouth watering. "Ok. I'll have that and a cup of coffee."

"I'll just have a cup of coffee," added William.

Earl cocked his head to the side and raised one eyebrow in a *You can't be serious* look.

A wide smile spread across William's face. "Just kidding. I'll have the same."

Earl shot a glance at the waitress who seemed agitated and didn't find any humor in William's jest. William didn't look and was apparently oblivious to her agitation."

"Is that all?" she asked in the same monotone voice. She barely waited for a response before she was off to another table.

"So, what's the favor I can do for you?" asked Earl.

William seemed very relaxed, and Earl sensed mild amusement from William at Earl's getting down to business attitude before they even had a cup of coffee.

"You like to get straight to the point, don't you? Ok. On Christmas Eve, we have a live nativity scene followed by a worship service. I was hoping that you would invite your congregation to our church and that you would do the sermon. People have heard me do it enough. I'd like them to hear a sermon from someone who is known for good sermons."

The request wasn't a strange one. Earl had done this before on special occasions like Easter where one church congregation was invited to another church to hear that church's pastor deliver the sermon. "I'd be honored, but are you sure? You heard my lackluster first sermon."

William seemed nonplussed. "I'm certain. I'm really looking forward to it. I'm glad I didn't have to try too hard to convince you."

The waitress set a cup of coffee in front of each man, and then rushed off at the call of someone from another table.

The comment that Samantha Estes made the previous day fleeted through Earl's mind. "By the way, the owner here, Samantha, had a great idea about having a homecooked Christmas meal for anyone with food insecurity. She said she would help provide the food, and maybe some of the other restaurants could as well. What do you think? Having it on Christmas Day may not seem ideal, but that might be the best time to show those in the community who are less fortunate that they aren't being forgotten on Christmas."

William shot his eyes up from adding sugar and creamer to his coffee. A look of unmitigated enthusiasm shone in his eyes. "That's a wonderful idea! I can check with the owner of Churchdale Barbeque, and the owner of the Pinewood Pizza Parlor goes to Victorious Life Church. I can ask her."

"Do you think Christmas Day is a good day to have it, or is it asking too much of people, especially those cooking the food?"

"I agree with what you said earlier. What better day to have something for those in need than on Christmas Day? I think people will come together for a good cause."

The waitress set their plates in front of them and rushed off without asking if everything looked ok. That was fine with Earl. Who really knew if everything was to their liking from a brief glimpse? Earl grabbed his fork as though it were a cut and polished diamond lying around just waiting to be snatched. He noticed William looking at him. "I'm sorry. I've barely eaten since arriving here. I have much to be thankful for in this meal."

William smiled. "If you have that much to be thankful for, between the two of us, you would be the best in asking the blessing for our food."

Earl was impressed with the way William handled the situation. Although William hadn't been in the ministry as long was Earl, Earl felt there was a lot he could learn from this young lion.

With a full belly from the large plate of food that stretched his shrunken stomach, Earl waddled to the door of the diner. He felt gluttonous, having eaten every bit of food on his plate while William only ate half as much. Earl opened the door, and the singing fish on the wall began singing Jingle Bells. Earl had heard it over and over as he ate and wondered if he was the only one in the diner who grew more and more annoyed by the member of the genus Micropterus. He jokingly conspired with William as to how they could secretly remove the annoying creature from the diner without being detected. Earl codenamed it Operation Large Mouth Bass.

Outside of the diner, Earl's stomach did a somersault, and he had to force the food back down. Earl grimaced at the cause of this reflux when he recognized Richard Coldwell walking out of a pharmacy walking away from them. Earl stopped dead in his tracks, causing William to accidentally bump into him.

"Is something wrong?" questioned William. "You look like you've seen the Ghost of Christmas Future."

Earl faltered. "I may have ... at least the Ghost of Christmas Past."

"Huh?"

Earl noticed the perplexed look on William's face. "Never mind ... It's nothing."

Chapter Thirteen

For several hours, Earl contemplated seeing Richard Coldwell. He knew it would happen sooner or later and was surprised that it had not occurred sooner. He had tried to prepare for the meeting. Still, the sighting had caught him off guard. And it wasn't even a meeting, just a sighting. What would happen when he actually came face to face with his nemesis?

Earl put it out of his mind as darkness descended. He wanted to enjoy the night with Harmony and not be distracted by his imagination running wild over this tormentor. The downtown area was quintessential Christmas as everyone prepared for the candlelight event. Harmony showed up dressed for the cold weather, complete with scarf, hat, and mittens, although this night wasn't as cold as the day they distributed flyers throughout the town. They each took a candle and promenaded down main street with the group of candle bearers. The night was clear, and stars dotted the sky, adding a special reverence for the event while complementing the town's Christmas lights and decorations. Booths were set up along the way with vendors selling hot chocolate, hot apple cider, and pickup snacks.

"Have you ever done this before?" asked Earl.

"No, but I like it. It's very peaceful."

"It is. I hope I didn't put you on the spot by asking you to come. I don't want a jealous boyfriend coming after me." Earl knew he was being transparent in asking the question, but he had been wondering for a while if Harmony had a boyfriend whom she was keeping secret. He did not look at Harmony when he asked the question. Being transparent was one thing. Being overly anxious was another.

"No boyfriend," she replied nonchalantly.

Earl glanced at her as she answered but quickly diverted his gaze from Harmony, fixing it instead on the vendors lining the street.

"Don't you remember how excited Samantha was when she thought you were my boyfriend? And I've told you about my experience with dating ... Also, not being old and having a great personality doesn't help."

Finally, Harmony had set him up to deliver his line. "Being beautiful though, I would think you'd have men lining up to ask you out."

Harmony leaned in and hooked Earl's arm with hers. "Now that's a great compliment! Too bad it took you so long to come up with it."

Was she flirting with him again? Or was she as interested in him as he was in her? They walked quietly, arm in arm. Earl felt peace that he had rarely felt since coming back to Pinewood.

"What about you? I know you're not married, but do you have a girlfriend?"

Earl took heart at the question. Maybe she was interested in him. "People in my former churches never tired of trying to set me up with a friend of a friend of a cousin, but blind dates never seemed to work out well."

"That's not an answer," she teased.

"No, is the direct answer to your question. But people look at me like I'm flawed when I give that answer."

Harmony gave him a playful shove. "There you go. You give a compliment and then undo it. If you're flawed because you don't have a girlfriend, you're insinuating that I'm flawed for not having a boyfriend."

Earl winced inside at his faux pas. Quickly he ran several comebacks through his brain until one stuck. "Well, you know … your career gives some insight regarding your personality that tends to turn men off."

She gave him another playful shove. This time he looked into her eyes, eyes that sparkled from the colors of lights that tantalizingly danced around her eyes, giving them a warm and inviting glow. Her eyes smiled, radiating the smile down to her mouth. "Was that a joke? Did Mr. Serious actually make a joke?" The smile turned into a laugh that warmed him more than anything the vendors were pedaling. "I know what you mean though about blind dates." She stopped before she could take the conversation further, and Earl followed her eyes to one of the numerous stands, one that was selling Christmas cookies. "Ooh. These look good. Do you want a Christmas cookie?"

"Sure." Earl paid the vendor for two cookies, iced to perfection. "With a candle in one hand, this sure is a good way to keep from overeating during the holidays."

To his chagrin, Harmony changed the subject to their church-related task. "I was wondering how we're going to collect, transport, and set up the Christmas trees. I'm sure we can get a few people in the congregation to help, but the work might be a little much for the older members, and the younger members work. We may need more than a few people."

Although Earl was dismayed at the turn of the conversation, he knew it was a topic that needed to be addressed sooner rather than later. He sighed audibly. "I know. And I don't want to have to ask Pastor Lorie for additional help, even though he would probably be glad to do so."

"Do you have any ideas then?"

"Perhaps." He did have an idea, but it had been a long time to ask this of someone he hadn't seen or spoken to in years. "Jerry has a truck with a trailer. Hopefully, he will let us use it. How flexible are your working hours tomorrow?"

"I told the assistant manager that I was taking some vacation days, and she'll cover for me."

Harmony wore a curious expression, and if Earl could have read her mind, he would have guessed that she wanted to tease his idea out into the open. "Meet me at the church tomorrow, and we'll see if my idea pays off."

"Secretive, are we? That's not a good quality in a date." She quickly added, "Not that I meant this was a date."

Earl felt he should be bold, else he might be headed for the friend zone. "I hope it is. It's been a while since I've been on a date with a not so old woman with a great personality ... who happens to be beautiful."

Harmony cocked her head at the comment and narrowed her eyes, almost as if focusing on Earl to see if he were serious. Her eyes twinkled, and the corners of her mouth moved upward just a few millimeters. Earl didn't think she was displeased by his comment. The way she said, "Hmm," sort of high-pitched, in a curious, almost questioning tone was interesting. Earl took it as an encouraging sign. He didn't know why. Trying to interpret *hmm* wasn't a science by any means.

The next day, Jerry was already at the church with his truck and trailer when Earl arrived. Earl had called him the previous night to see if he would be available, and he felt fortunate that Jerry was retired and willing to help out on a moment's notice, if able. Earl was with Harmony when he called Jerry, and they worked out a time to meet.

While Earl waited for Harmony to arrive, he walked a short distance away to make a quick phone call. Not that Jerry would have heard him anyway; he was in his truck listening to the radio and keeping warm. Earl had been talking to the person on the other end of the line for a couple of minutes when Harmony pulled up. She got out of her car and walked over to Earl as he was finishing up his phone conversation.

"Thanks. I appreciate it. Hope to talk to you real soon," concluded Earl as he ended the call. "You look like a lumberjack," bantered Earl upon seeing Harmony wearing blue jeans, brown, ankle-high work boots, a flannel shirt, and a baseball cap.

Harmony gazed down at her clothes. "You said wear something to work in. When working with trees, what's more appropriate than dressing like a lumberjack? And by the way, I hope you meant lumberjill," she emphasized the *Jill* part. "I hope I don't look like a man!"

"Far from it. Poor choice of words. You actually look cute."

"Oh, so last night, you said I was beautiful. Have I already been demoted to cute?"

"I can't win, can I?"

"As long as you realize that, we're on good terms."

Jerry got out of his truck and ambled over to Earl and Harmony. "You two seem to be having a good time this morning."

"Just some back and forth banter, typical for us," declared Earl.

"You must be confident in your idea since Jerry has his truck and trailer here," exclaimed Harmony.

"The first step of faith is believing."

"What exactly is my role?" puzzled Jerry.

"You're going to wait here, and we'll call you if this pans out."

"Don't you mean when this pans out?" teased Harmony. "Faith. Remember?"

"When it pans out." Earl held the door open. "Hop in the car."

Earl drove to the mobile home development he passed by on the day he arrived in Pinewood. On the basketball court, a group of ten youth were playing basketball with several more watching on. Earl parked the car, and Harmony and he walked over and watched the youth play. It wasn't long before they attracted the attention of the onlookers, who were soon pointing and jeering. Earl couldn't hear what they were saying, and it was probably better that way.

"What are we doing here?" whispered Harmony.

"You'll see in a little bit."

When the youth on the court took a break, Earl ventured over with Harmony following closely.

"You've got a good game going," he called out to the youth. A few looked his way but then turned away. Meanwhile several of the onlookers were still jeering. "I'm Earl Stanley, Pastor of Pinewood Church."

One of the teens, a Latino youth who appeared to be the leader of the group swaggered over to Earl with his chest puffed out and his arms bowed back. A smirk, laced with a know-it-all cockiness, played across his mouth. "We're not coming to your church. You can go ahead and leave."

"I'm not here to invite you to church." Earl stated that in a way as though that were the furthest thing from his mind, and he paused and looked at the teen as if he were waiting for the young man to identify himself.

"Luis. The name's Luis." Luis appeared to be about sixteen years old. "I've never met a pastor yet who hasn't asked," replied Luis in a voice dripping with superiority.

"I have a proposition for all of you. We need some strong people to transport and set up trees for our Christmas Tree lot, and I was hoping you could help us."

Luis raised his head slightly and leaned forward, "Whachu gonna pay?"

"Seeing how we're going to use the profits for our Christmas drives, we can't really pay. Otherwise, we would eat into our profits." Earl looked around seeking understanding for his logic.

Luis snarled and dug his teeth into his lower lip. "Not interested." He turned his back to Earl and started to saunter off.

"Earl's voice rose higher into a pleading, almost questioning, pitch. "I'll buy pizza for everyone who helps."

Luis spun around, laughing. With a broad smile aimed at Earl, he raised his arms out to his sides, parallel to the ground with palms facing upward, and turned slowly. His self-assured behavior was a commanding presence that raptly held the attention of the other youth. Luis moved his fingers in a beckoning gesture, curling and uncurling them in tidal like periodicity. Like a maestro conducting an orchestra, he worked up the other youth until their taunts and jeers grew louder. Then, he howled in a mock preaching voice,

"Here that, guys and gals? *Preach* is going to buy us pizza in exchange for our hard work." The youth laughed loudly in unison.

Earl shot a quick glance at Harmony. Her posture was tense, but her body was antsy. Earl hoped he hadn't misjudged the youth's capacity for violent behavior. He wouldn't be able to forgive himself if any harm came to Harmony. Just as Earl thought Luis was going to incite the others further, Luis facial expression changed to irritation, and he dampened the heat with two words.

"Get lost."

Earl breathed a sigh of relief, having sidestepped potential disaster. It had been so long since he had been in the community that he had forgotten how people could behave. This had been a mild reminder of the potential for danger. Still, he hadn't come this far to flee in defeat. He dared to push a little harder. "I don't mind negotiating more. It looks like you could use two new basketball goals, and a lot of your shoes are looking pretty worn. What if I throw that in?"

Earl could see the curiosity on Luis' face and the surprise that Earl had not ran to his car and sped off.

"That will cost more than just paying us. Let me guess. The Lord will provide."

The others burst into laughter.

Earl was impressed at Luis' logic while still commanding the attention and behavior of the others.

Luis continued. "And I'll bet come Christmas Day, none of those promises will have materialized. And don't go asking don't we trust a preacher."

Earl was shocked at himself; he was actually enjoying the banter and the game the two were playing. "I can understand your skepticism, but you've got a lot to gain and not much to lose."

"We've heard that before," snapped Luis.

"As I said, let's negotiate. What would it take?" Earl was timorous over the question he had just asked. He wanted to guide Luis along a specific path, but in their game of chess, Luis could go in any number of directions.

The cocky smirk that Luis displayed earlier reappeared. "Get the shoes autographed by a pro basketball player and we'll do it, right guys?" Luis repeated the arm and hand gesture he had used earlier to once again work the group up into whoops and hollers.

Earl pulled out his phone, and everyone quieted. Luis stared at Earl with a mix of curiosity and incredulity. Earl touched his phone a few times. As he waited for his call to connect, he turned up the volume, turned on the speaker and moved toward Luis. "Hi, Jarrett. How charitable are you feeling for Christmas?"

A voice came through the speaker. "Pastor Earl! What can I do for you?"

Earl spoke with the calmness of a man in a grocery store who had just called his wife to ask about which product to buy. "I've got a group of young men and women who need two new basketball goals and about ... let me see sixteen pairs of new basketball shoes autographed by Christmas. In exchange, they're going to do some work for me to help with our Christmas drives."

"That's too easy. How about I come down and give some basketball pointers too?"

Earl began playing it up. "I don't know. This is a skeptical group, Jarrett. How about saying something to one of them? Hopefully, he'll recognize Jarrett Bridges' voice."

At the mention of the name *Jarrett Bridges*, all faces perked up, and everyone's attention was directed to the match being played before them. Earl handed the phone to Luis with the speaker still on.

"To whom am I speaking?" came the polite, deep, rich, voice of Jarrett Bridges.

The ostentatiousness in Luis' face had disappeared, but Earl knew that Luis still needed to save face with the others and that he would be skeptical.

"My name is Luis. If you're really Jarrett Bridges, what were your stats last year in the regular season?"

Jarrett must have expected the question. He rapidly rattled them off. "Seventy-five games played. Twenty-eight point seven points per game, fifty point six field goal percentage, forty point seven three-point percentage, nine point five assists per game, and ten point one rebounds per game. Convinced?"

Luis' jaw dropped, and he no longer seemed to be the raucous teen he had appeared mere moments earlier. "Yes. Mr. Bridges." Luis handed the phone to Earl. "We'll do it!"

Earl called Jerry to take his truck and trailer to Farmer Brown's farm, and he called William to bring the small bus without the church logo from Victorious Life Church. Earl had mentioned to William the previous night that he might need to transport a group of people, and William offered to provide transportation. Earl and Harmony sat in Earl's car as they waited for William to arrive.

"I don't believe what I just witnessed." Harmony sat still; her body still appeared tense. "Did you just wing all of that?"

"I'm not a magician. I spoke with Jarrett last night and again when you arrived at the church. I know Jarrett from a previous church I pastored. We just put on a little show."

"Well, I have to say. I'm still impressed, a little shaken, but impressed. If you think you've lost your touch at all of this, I can bear witness that that is not the case in any shape or form."

"Thank you," replied Earl. "But I am still a little rusty."

"You made it look as easy as riding bike after not having ridden one for years."

As they were talking, William drove up in the bus, and all the youth climbed in. Then Earl and Harmony tailed William as he drove to the farm, which was about a fifteen-minute drive from Pinewood.

At the farm, the trees had already been cut. All the youth had to do was haul the cut trees to the trailer. Once they transported them to the church, Harmony directed the group of teens as they set up the Christmas trees in the church yard. Earl knew he had gone to a lot of trouble to accomplish something he could have accomplished without the pomp and the time it took to elicit the help of the teens, but he hoped to accomplish more than simply transporting cut trees from the farm to the church. He had been out of practice; it had been around eleven years since he had done something similar, but he liked the feeling he was experiencing. He had forgotten that feeling and had assumed that it would never return again.

As promised, after the hard work they put in, Earl took them to the Pinewood Pizza Parlor. The pizza parlor wasn't overly crowded, but several heads turned as the large group of teens bound into the restaurant. The aroma of freshly baked pizza filled the air, causing excited chatter among the teens. A few of the youth had never had pizza, and they cast surreptitious glances to those around them who seemed to know how to eat this strange food. Earl was momentarily surprised that some of them had never eaten pizza. Some had never been to a restaurant before, and they were receiving tutoring from some of the others on how to behave inside the restaurant. No wonder going out to eat pizza didn't seem like a big deal to them back at the basketball court. Earl had forgotten what the poorer mobile home neighborhoods were like, and he was getting a quick reminder. They occupied several tables and ate more pizza than Earl anticipated. He had forgotten the appetites that teenagers had.

The teens' laughter and chatter grew louder as they relaxed and adjusted to the atmosphere at the pizza parlor. Stories and jokes effused the air. On one occasion, the group grew a little louder than Earl was comfortable with, but the staff seemed friendly enough. Occasionally they would glance over, seemingly happy to see the youths enjoying the outing.

Earl sat next to Luis, who voraciously dug into the pizza. After several pieces, he opened up about his background. His mother had moved to the mobile home neighborhood from a nearby town when he was seven years old, after Luis' father left. His mother juggled several jobs to try to provide for him and his younger sister who was three years younger than him. She was one of the ones at the table who stole glances at how to eat pizza. Luis said he often played hooky from school. He didn't see the point in going; he was probably going to have to drop out within a year to begin doing odd jobs to help support the family. His mother grew more and more haggard and tired with each passing day, and he didn't know how much longer she could keep up working multiple jobs. To say that Earl was dismayed by Luis' story was an understatement. His heart ached for the family. Luis was smart, maybe not book smart, although Earl sensed he could be very easily, and Earl didn't want to see him throw his future away and struggle to make ends meet the way his mother was having to do. Luis seemed to have a soft, caring heart despite the rough exterior he displayed.

Earl made his way around, talking with as many of the youth as possible. Each story he heard tugged at his heart, reminding him of why he chose the ministry in the first place. It wasn't to deliver sermons or preach to people. As his nightmare reminded him, he had joined the ministry because he believed that the best way to show God's love was to reach out to those in need and meet them where they were.

Maria, a shy, brown-skinned girl with dark hair and dark, expressive eyes, sat quietly, guarding and savoring her slice of pizza. She had eaten pizza before, but it had been years ago. Her family moved to the mobile home neighborhood about four years ago after the bank foreclosed on their home. Harmony seemed especially disturbed by the story because it was the bank she was now branch manager of that foreclosed on the family's house, although she didn't tell Maria this.

Thomas, who went by Tommy, was a tall, lanky sixteen-year-old who was one of the better basketball players. He lived with his grandmother. Neither she nor he knew where his mother was. She had fallen victim to drug abuse, and his grandmother kicked his mother out several years ago. His father had served in the U.S. Air Force and was killed in a freak accident while he was stationed in North Dakota.

"You have all lost a lot," emphasized Earl. "But the one thing you haven't lost is each other."

The youth smiled and began talking happily again. Earl was amazed at the transformation from rowdy teens to people feeling a sense of accomplishment. The struggles they faced had not beaten them down, yet. He knew that as time went by that would probably not be the case for a lot of these youth. Earl wanted to help, but it would take more than new basketball goals and basketball shoes to do that. Despite their struggles, tonight was a time to temporarily step outside of them. Everyone ate, talked, and laughed as though they had known each other for years.

By the end of the evening at the pizza parlor, Earl sensed that this had been more than a partial payment for the work the youth did that day. It had turned into a time of connection and possibly bonding. What had been a treat for the youth was a mixed bag for Earl. It certainly was a treat for him, and he enjoyed getting to know the group of teens beyond the taunts they had flung his way earlier. But it was also a reminder of the reason Earl had become a pastor in the first place and a painful jolt to him for the person he had become since leaving Pinewood. His dream of being a pastor at a megachurch seemed trivial when compared to the work that he could be doing. Yet, despite this jarring reality-check, he knew in his heart that he was not capable of sustaining this type of day-to-day outreach. The nightmare of his failure always loomed in the shadows of his soul, ready to strike out at any moment. And pastoring a megachurch was important too, wasn't it? There were lives everywhere that could benefit by a preaching ministry. Earl pushed the dilemma out of his mind. For now, he would simply bask in the new connections he had made.

Chapter Fourteen

Earl had been worried that the trees wouldn't sell, but they had a crowd of people picking out trees in the makeshift tree lot. Christmas music played in the background, and several of the youth from the mobile home neighborhood helped wrap and load trees. Jerry showed them how to tie appropriate knots in the twine used to tie trees to the tops of cars.

William Lorie walked up as Earl finished collecting money from a customer.

"Word is out around town of what you've done. It's truly amazing."

Those words meant a lot to Earl. "It felt good to get out from behind the pulpit again."

"If you'll excuse me, I'm going to pick out a tree."

Earl was startled by the appearance of Ted Long, who seemed to have materialized out of thin air.

"You're off to a great start, Pastor. Remember what we said though about getting the right number of trees. We don't want to be stuck with a lot left over, and remember to update us regularly."

On the surface, nothing seemed wrong in anything Ted said. But Earl still felt he was being lectured to and micromanaged. Why couldn't he have simply stopped with, *You're off to a good start?*

Images of Richard Coldwell's past criticisms flooded Earl's mind. Earl was not a prognosticator. How was he supposed to know the exact number of trees needed? And Ted seemed more concerned that too many trees would be left over than not enough.

Later that night, Earl and Harmony were the only two people remaining, and only one tree was left in the lot.

"One tree left," declared Earl. "We did a good day's work."

"Correction. No trees left. I'm buying the last one for you. The parsonage doesn't look very Christmassy. We need to remedy that."

"Thank you, but I don't have any decorations."

A sly smile formed on Harmony's face. "I figured as much. That's why I brought some with me."

"You don't intend that we decorate tonight, do you?"

"It's not that late, and it won't take long. Besides, I have tomorrow off. Do you have somewhere special you need to be tomorrow that you can't sleep in an extra hour in the morning if you need to?"

"No. Not really."

"Then let's get busy decorating your tree!"

The last remaining tree was not one of the larger ones. Still, it had lush, full branches, and the tree was fairly symmetrical. Fortunately, Harmony predicted that Earl wouldn't have a tree stand either, and she had brought one along. Earl, with Harmony's direction adjusted the tree so that it stood straight. Harmony selected a Christmas playlist that played traditional Christmas songs as they decorated. They wrapped several strands of clear lights around the tree; Harmony occasionally stepped back, observed the lights, and made slight adjustments to minimize gaps. Earl plugged in the lights, and they stood back to admire the tree. The room was filled with the soft glow of fairy lights.

Next, Harmony opened the lid of the plastic container containing ornaments. She picked one up, the bauble reflecting the twinkling lights from the tree. Harmony laughed at the haphazard way Earl hung the ornaments, and she traded positions with him.

The conversation flowed easily between them as they decorated the tree. Harmony shared childhood memories of helping her parents decorate the tree.

"I haven't put up a Christmas tree in the past few years," shared Earl.

Harmony shot a surprised look his way.

"Well, it's been just me, and I didn't feel the need to put up one. Besides, no one usually came over anyway during the Christmas season. People would usually invite me to their homes."

"I'm not judging. I'm just a little surprised."

Harmony didn't have a ton of decorations; so, she was correct in that it didn't take too long to decorate the tree. Once they finished putting up the ornaments, Earl stood back to admire their teamwork. He sniffed a deep breath of the pine scent that filled the room, and Harmony laughed at the loud sniffing sound he made.

"It's beautiful," beamed Earl.

"We're not done decorating yet though."

Earl scoured the floor for other decorations. "Isn't that all of the decorations?"

"You're forgetting the star." Harmony pulled a star out of a bag from behind a chair that Earl had missed seeing.

"I have a small stepladder in the other room. Let me fetch it, and I'll be right back." Earl disappeared momentarily and came back with the stepladder. He set it up next to the tree. Before he could grab the star from Harmony, she was already bounding up the stepladder with the star. She put the star on top of the tree and made some minor adjustments before she was satisfied with its placement.

She began descending the stepladder as quickly as she had bound up it but missed a step in her haste. She cried out, and although Earl was already there, he instinctively opened his arms to catch her. As she fell, she twisted in midair and landed in Earl's firm embrace, face-to-face with him.

Earl kept a firm grip on her as she steadied herself. His hands slid to her upper arms, near her shoulders ensuring she was stable and free from injury from her corkscrew fall. Harmony exhaled sharply, her hand flying to her chest. She looked up, and Earl locked his eyes onto hers.

"Are you alright?" he asked softly, his voice tinged with concern.

Harmony nodded, and a faint blush crept from her throat slowly to her cheeks. "Thank you," she replied in a breathy, shaken voice.

Earl stood there, looking into her warm eyes, unable to let her go. The world around him faded, until nothing remained but Harmony. Slowly, he became aware of his senses. His breathing was short and shallow, but he couldn't force himself to take in deeper breaths. His heart danced rapidly, and he could hear it beating in his ears. Her face was all he could see and all he wanted to see. He yearned to touch her angelic face until the desire was uncontrollable. With the palm of his hand and his fingertips, he touched her soft skin, tracing her face, first her cheek and then her chin. The smell of fresh pine emanated from her. All that remained was the sense of taste. He desperately wanted to taste her lips. He could barely think, but he wondered if she was as mesmerized as he was. Apparently, she was. Slowly, as if by some unseen force, their lips inched closer, stopping short of a kiss as an ornament dropped from the tree, shattering on the floor, and breaking the spell they were under. The electric charge in the air began to dissipate. Harmony breathed the slightest laugh and softly bit her lip. In a slow retreat, she slid her arms across his shoulders and ran her hands along his chest as she inched away, avoiding eye contact.

"Well, I imagine it's late. I suppose I need to leave. I'll clean up the broken ornament first though."

The words soured at Earl's ears, but he knew she was right. "Don't worry about the ornament. I'll get it."

She turned, still avoiding looking into his eyes. She took a few determined steps and stopped. "What's this?"

Earl was still a few seconds behind, living in the moment of the almost kiss, before he realized she had spoken. Earl forced the daydreams from his mind until it had cleared enough to register what Harmony was talking about.

She was looking at the piece of paper with the one sentence printed on it that Earl had tossed on the table and forgotten.

"Oh." The sound of his voice seemed to further clear the residue from his mind, and he was now fully in the present. "Someone left it at my door the night after I preached that awful first sermon. I don't know if it's a prank or if someone was trying to cheer me up. I haven't received anything yet. My guess is that it was a prank."

"I feel a little jealous. Do you have another woman in the congregation giving you gifts?"

Her voice sounded playful, causing Earl to wonder whether she really was jealous or just teasing. Being unsure of her intent, he was unsure of how to reply. When he did, his voice was flat and devoid of emotion. "Definitely not … I wondered at one time if it were you who put it at my door."

"Not me. Interesting." Harmony's voice seemed to mirror his own.

While Earl was wondering how to determine if she really liked him or not, he noticed he was talking. It was as if his mind were operating independently from him. "Would you like to come over for dinner tomorrow night? It won't be anything extravagant. I'd love the company."

Harmony glanced up at him. "It's a date ..." She quickly glanced away and softly bit her lip again before continuing. "Only if you want it to be."

Earl smiled. "It's a date." After crossing paths with Harmony, William, and Luis, perhaps some of their confidence was beginning to rub off on him.

Chapter Fifteen

Earl arrived late at the church the next day, having slept in a little longer. Then he left early to go buy groceries and begin preparing dinner for Harmony and him. He told her dinner wouldn't be anything extravagant, and he was right. Spaghetti, breadsticks, and salad was what he finally decided on. There wasn't much he could screw up on with that meal.

Harmony wore a green dress that matched the festive season. The dress was quite the contrast from the tree lot attire of the previous day. Earl wasn't sure how to dress but went with a business casual look of dress pants and a dress shirt.

As they were eating, Earl was having second thoughts about the meal he had prepared. He was almost certain he would have spaghetti sauce on his shirt before the meal was over. At least he wasn't wearing a white shirt.

After the *almost kiss* from last night, Earl was finding it difficult to make small talk. Earl and Harmony were quiet for most of the meal. Finally, when both had almost finished, Earl broke the silence. "I told you it wouldn't be extravagant."

"It's delicious. Do you cook a lot?"

"Some, but not a lot. At bigger churches, there always seems to be a meal for various occasions, and families tend to invite me over often. A lot of families want to talk about the church though, especially since I don't have a family. The conversations get old after a while."

Harmony put down her fork and saluted. "Got it. No church talk."

"Well ..." The way he said *well* apparently aroused her attention.

"Is there something about the church you want to talk about?"

Earl frowned, pushing the remaining food around on his plate. "You know how when people see accidents, they can't help but look. I feel sort of the same way. I tried to forget about what happened to me at Pinewood and to completely forget about Pinewood Church. But it's haunted me ever since. What happened after I left?"

Harmony finished the last bite of food and swallowed hard. Her eyes darted from side to side, and Earl wondered what she was thinking. She wiped her hands on the cloth napkin and dabbed it to each corner of her mouth before she spoke. "The church pretty much imploded. Several of the wealthier families left; some have never returned to church. The remaining group moved to the current location. The land and former location were sold to the barbecue restaurant and the remaining group purchased the current church."

Earl fidgeted with his food some more. Then realizing he was playing the part of a five-year old at the dinner table, stood up. Harmony instinctively rose as well, and they both meandered into the living room. Harmony sat on the couch, but Earl paced back and forth.

"What about the mobile home park and the people who lived there?"

Harmony leaned back and watched Earl parade in front of the couch. "A few months after you left, a bad storm came through, and lightning struck one of the mobile homes in the park. Several homes burned. The landowner sold the land, and the housing development gentrified the neighborhood. The people who were there moved to the mobile home neighborhood where you met the youth playing basketball.

Earl stopped pacing. "All of my work here was for nothing."

Harmony furrowed her brow. First of all, that's not true. You did help people, and the old Pinewood Church was living on borrowed time no matter who the pastor would have been. Second, I just now told you what happened, but it's been obvious that something has been bothering you for years. Out with it."

Harmony spoke with such insight and such a commanding presence that Earl felt compelled to tell her. Earl looked up at the ceiling, and his mind took him back to that time. He began slowly, like and old man reflecting on what he had done with his life. "I had so much energy when I started pastoring." Earl stopped and searched his mind for that image, an image that was buried deeply in the crevices of his mind and hard to find. He searched for a purpose that he no longer had. "I felt that the church was to help the community it was in. Pinewood Church was almost right next to the mobile home community of poor and disenfranchised people. I felt we needed to help, not by bringing them in to preach to them but by going out amongst them." The room began to fade, as if Earl had been transported back to that time. "I wanted to teach them first aid and healthy habits. I wanted to provide fellowship for those who didn't get out. I wanted to teach the youth the joys there were in life whether it was in music or playing ball or helping others."

"And didn't you do that?"

Earl glanced at Harmony and saw the perplexed look on her face. It was the same perplexed look William had had on his face when he mentioned to Earl that he had heard about all the good Earl had done in the community when he was last in Pinewood. How could he share with Harmony what he felt in a way that she would understand? "I did, but my efforts displeased the leaders and established families in the church, especially the lead layperson, Richard Coldwell. They felt I neglected the church I was sent here to serve and, in the process, let wolves in amongst the sheep."

"Do you really believe that?"

"I do ... or did ... maybe I still do." Rather than gaining clarity from this conversation with Harmony, he felt as confused as ever. "I lost all my confidence in doing outreach ministry. I've barely done any. I focused my energy on delivering sermons. I didn't want to ignore the congregation like I was accused of doing here."

"Faith without works is dead. But you know that. As a pastor you can't choose one or the other; you have to do both."

Earl told her about his recurring nightmare, going into vivid details. He explained how it had chronically affected him. "Sometimes, I wonder if I have Post-Traumatic Stress Disorder. The bishop says I have Imposter Syndrome." He stopped talking and shot another look in Harmony's direction to see if she understood what he was feeling. Instead, he witnessed a look that startled him. He saw the tension in Harmony's body. Her hands clutched her green dress at her knees. She looked paralyzed. It was a look that seemed to him that she was in the room with a different person than the one she thought she knew. At that moment, he felt as though he had lost her for good. He said too much. He had dumped the dirty laundry of his baggage out in the open for someone to see, and he knew it wasn't a pretty sight. If she hadn't seemed paralyzed, he wouldn't have been surprised in the least if she got up and sprinted to the door, fleeing from a psycho.

Harmony's mouth started to form a question, and her uneasiness at asking it was apparent to Earl. "Are you scared of Richard Coldwell? He wasn't a physical threat. He may have been a bully, but he wasn't the devil incarnate. I know you know the power of words, but words can't hurt you unless you let them."

Earl could clearly see what Harmony thought of him. "So, you think I'm a coward." He said it so mater-of-factly that it was like a blow to Harmony, knocking her back against the couch and jolting her mind from whatever it had been thinking. She leaned forward, looking down, her eyes playing dodgeball with an imaginary ball.

After a few seconds, Harmony stood up and determinedly strode to Earl. She took his hands into hers and looked deeply into his eyes. "I think you are a man with a lot of heart. A man that God wants to use. I think you've been struggling by yourself and with yourself to find your way back to the man God wants you to be again." She reached up, putting her hands on Earl's chest and kissed him gently on the lips. I didn't mean to insult you. I was just trying to understand."

"It's hard for me to expect you to understand me when I don't understand myself. A stray thought planted itself in Earl's mind. "Before I left to come here, an eight-year-old girl gave me a great insight into myself. She pointed out that almost everything I've done as a minister, I've done by myself without involving others. The bishop sent me here to regain my confidence in doing outreach and face my demons. From the insight of a child, I knew that I needed to involve others this time."

"That's why you're letting me help and why you called Jarrett Bridges."

"That's not entirely the reason I'm letting you help. I enjoy spending time with you." The realization of his emotion dump, and how it must have appeared to Harmony, was setting in. He regretted every bit of what he had said. "I'm sorry. I didn't invite you over here to dump on you. Now, I promise to change the subject. Unfortunately, I didn't make dessert."

"What? No dessert?"

Earl could tell that Harmony was trying to lighten the mood, but he could tell by her voice that she was obviously bothered by what he said. "I'm sorry about the dessert."

"It's okay. I have to cover for the assistant manager early tomorrow morning; so, I need to leave anyway. Thanks for dinner. I'll see you tomorrow night for the hayride."

Earl heard Harmony's car start and pull out of the driveway. "What did I just do?" Earl knew he let the cat out of the bag, and there was no putting it back.

Earl went to bed, but he had a horrible night. He drifted in and out of sleep. It was one of those nights that he wasn't sure if he was asleep or awake. He replayed the night's event over and over through his mind. He finally drifted off to sleep and had a bad dream. It wasn't his recurring nightmare, but it was troubling, nonetheless. In his dream, Richard Coldwell was the captain of a sailing ship in the 1700s. Earl was the boatswain, and he had not taken proper care of the sails. Earl was tied to the mast without his shirt. Richard made a showy display, and he had a bag from which he withdrew a cat o' nine tails whip. With the cat out of the bag, Earl heard Richard say, "ten lashes." Earl braced himself for the first lash. He looked to his right and saw Harmony with a look of horror on her face. Earl awoke from the dream, and several hours passed before he fell asleep again.

Chapter Sixteen

The farm oozed a traditional Christmas spirit for the hayride. Farmer Brown used this area as a venue for various events to supplement his income: Halloween, Christmas, weddings, and retreats. Tonight, he wasn't charging the church a penny. Earl had arrived early in case he needed to help, but Farmer Brown, a generous and jovial man, had everything covered. Earl returned to the church to coordinate the transportation to the farm.

The first bus arrived, dropped off its cargo of people and departed to pick up another group. Others arrived in their own cars or trucks.

The night was perfect for the event. A slight chill tinged the night air, and each person's breath formed a tiny cloud in an otherwise cloudless night that displayed a dazzling view of the moon and stars, undiminished by any light from the town. Twinkling lights decorated the barn, and several uncut live trees near the barn were adorned with lights and decorations. The aroma of pine mingled with rich chocolate, fresh-baked cookies, and hot popcorn. Christmas music played softly in the background.

A tractor's engine rumbled as it approached a crowd of eager people waiting in line for a ride. The first group climbed in, some with blankets wrapped around them, and found spots to sit amongst the bales of hay. The tractor chugged through an open field before disappearing into a pine forest.

Back at the barn, Farmer Brown, dressed as Santa Claus, helped hand out steaming cups of hot chocolate topped with whipped cream and dusted with nutmeg. At other times, he took pictures with children. Inside, the barn had been transformed into a makeshift movie theater. Families and groups sat in folding chairs or propped themselves up against bales of hay and munched on popcorn as they watched movies. *Home Alone* was shown first, followed by *Elf.*

Earl performed a variety of jobs that night: parking attendant, hot chocolate server, popcorn popper, and even housekeeping. Harmony, Jerry, and a few others from the church also took turns at various jobs.

Finally, the last vehicle left, leaving only Earl and Harmony remaining. Earl felt exhausted, and he was sure Harmony felt that way as well. Earl and Harmony were alone. It felt awkward, especially because he didn't know where they stood after last night. He had barely spoken to Harmony that night; both had been so busy.

As he wondered what to say, Harmony broke the ice. "I told my parents that you hadn't had many homecooked meals since you arrived back in Pinewood." She winked at Earl. "They asked if you cooked, and I told you were having to relearn because everyone at your last church took care of you. They would like for you to come over for dinner tomorrow night, if you're not busy."

"I won't be too proud. If my lack of cooking skills will get me a free dinner, I'm glad to take it."

"Great. I'll text you the address."

Farmer Brown, still dressed as Santa, ambled up to Earl and Harmony.

"I think you two were the only ones who didn't get a chance to go on a hayride. Climb in, and I'll take you myself."

"We don't want to put you to the trouble," declared Earl.

"Nonsense. Climb in. You don't want to disappoint Santa, do you? You might end up on the naughty list."

"Well, in that case, we'd love to go," beamed Harmony.

Earl climbed into the wagon first, and then he helped Harmony in. Earl plopped against a bale of hay, and Harmony crawled in next to him. She shivered and cuddled against Earl. "Here. Let's get under this blanket." Earl snatched the blanket and spread it across them both. Farmer Brown glanced back and smiled at the two. Then he cranked the tractor, and the tractor chugged through the field.

"It's really peaceful out here," cooed Harmony. "I'm glad it's just the two of us." She smiled and looked into Earl's eyes. Earl found Harmony's hand beneath the blanket, and their fingers intertwined. They leaned back against the hay, Harmony's head on Earl's shoulder, and they looked up at the moon and stars on this peaceful night.

The trepidation that Earl had of losing Harmony after the previous night's revelation began to fade. It disappeared completely when Harmony confessed, "This has been the best Christmas season I've had in a long time."

"Me too!" exclaimed Earl.

They leaned in, their lips touching, and they kissed as the tractor rumbled and bounced through the woods.

Chapter Seventeen

Earl put the directions that Harmony had given him to her parents' house into his car's GPS. According to the map, her parents only lived a few miles outside of town. As Earl drove, he tried to remember her parents from his previous stint at Pinewood Church. He had looked up the picture of the family from the old church directory. Harmony's father was Hank Waters, and her mother was Elaine. His mind held a vague memory of her parents. Although he remembered them from the church, he couldn't remember any specific memories, and nothing special stuck out.

The drive to the house was only about ten to fifteen minutes. Earl guessed that the house was built in the 1990s and at one time had been the only house around. A few newer-looking houses stood nearby, but Harmony's parents' house still stood on a spacious plot of land, surrounded by rolling hills and woodland. The house looked to be a single-story ranch style house, but it included elements of a colonial style. The exterior was predominantly brick with a gabled roof and a wide front porch supported by white columns. The porch had a porch swing and rocking chairs. Flower beds lined the front of the house, separated by brick steps leading up to the porch.

Earl walked onto the front porch and rang the doorbell. Earl recognized Elaine when she opened the door, and his nose was greeted by the tantalizing aroma of a home-cooked meal, making his mouth water and his stomach rumble.

"Hello, Pastor. Please come in. Let me take your coat."

Earl walked into the spacious foyer with its hardwood flooring. He handed his coat to Elaine. She looked much the same as her picture. Time had been good to her.

"Thank you for inviting me. I hope Harmony didn't make me sound too pitiful when it comes to eating. It's true that I have had to cook more, but it's been coming back to me."

Elaine smiled, not really giving Earl a clear response to his statement. Harmony's father, Hank, appeared from around the corner. He did look a decade older than his picture, but Harmony said he had suffered a heart attack around a year ago. That had to have had some effect on his appearance, but he still looked to be a strong man with rough hands and a leather-lined face.

"Come into the living room and have a seat," motioned Elaine. "Dinner is almost ready, and Harmony will be out momentarily."

Earl took a seat on one end of an L-shaped sofa, and Hank and Elaine sat on the other end of the other side of the L-shaped sofa. Earl regretted that Harmony was apparently getting ready. He would have to engage in small talk until she came in.

"How have you found Pinewood since you've returned?" asked Elaine.

"It's grown some, but for the most part, it still seems much the same."

After Earl's answer, there was a period of awkward silence. Elaine straightened her dress; Hank wore a neutral expression and stared at a television that wasn't turned on. The silence bit into Earl's nerves until he could no longer stand it, and it urged him to say something. The first thing he could think of saying was church-related. "So, do you go to Pinewood Church or another church?" Earl regretted it as soon as the words left his mouth.

Elaine blurted out almost involuntarily, "We haven't been to church in years." She hesitated. "It's just that ... we ..."

Earl interrupted before she could go further. "This is not a confessional; you don't have to explain." He had tried to make a joke out of it, but it fell flat.

Elaine ignored Earl and continued to try to explain. "During the church's time of trouble ... "

Earl appreciated the way that Elaine had tactfully referred to the church's implosion as a time of trouble. Her expression took Earl back to seminary when Professor Goodpaster spoke of the time of Jacob's trouble from the Book of Jeremiah. Of course, her sugarcoating was unnecessary; Earl knew she was referring to the schism he had caused within Pinewood Church.

Elaine's conversation brought Earl back to the present. "So, we haven't been to church since."

Hank expounded on what his wife was trying to say without hurting Earl's feelings. It was the first time since he arrived that Hank had spoken. My ancestors helped build Pinewood Church. That was what inspired me to become a contractor. There was a stone outside of the building that had the builders' family surnames listed. The name *Waters* was on that stone. The stone is not at the old church location anymore. I guess the owner of Churchdale Barbeque got rid of it. It's a shame the church is a barbeque joint now. Elaine wanted to go to the new church because her family had been a part of Pinewood Church. She didn't want to go anywhere else. My family had been a part of Pinewood Church too, but I couldn't bring myself to go to the new location. To me, it just wasn't the same church. I tried to compromise. I suggested another church, but Elaine wouldn't have it. As Elaine said, we haven't been to church since."

What could Earl say to that? Nothing. Nothing but change the subject, and Earl so blatantly changed the subject that it would have been quite comical to anyone watching. "So, Elaine, I don't remember what your profession was."

"I'm retired now, but I was a teacher at the middle school."

"Everywhere we go, people tell her what a great teacher she was." Hank seemed proud of his wife's accomplishments."

"It's the same with Hank," added Elaine. "He was a working contractor and helped build a lot of people's houses in the community, including ours. He probably would have continued if he had not had a heart attack last year."

"I have a woodworking shop in the backyard. I enjoy spending time out there and working on various projects."

"We're so thankful that Harmony came back to help after Hank had his heart attack. She's been a real blessing. I don't know what we would have done without her. We were especially excited when she moved in with us rather than getting a place of her own. I know it's hard to move in with one's parents at her age. I know she wants to get a job at the bank's corporate headquarters. We, of course, want her to realize her dreams, but we'll definitely miss her if she leaves."

"Did I hear my name?" Harmony entered the room, and Earl was not only thankful she arrived, but he was more thankful that she took her time getting ready. She was beautiful, and it was well worth the wait."

"What were you all talking about?" asked Harmony.

"We were talking about why we no longer go to church," replied Hank in a matter-of-fact manner.

A shocked expression instantly appeared on Harmony's face, and she glanced at Earl for confirmation. "Dad! You didn't need to tell all of that to the Pastor."

"He asked," confessed Hank.

Harmony shot an equally shocked expression toward Earl. All he could do was simply shrug his shoulders in a *don't ask* manner. Harmony quickly changed the subject. "So, mom, did you tell Earl what's for dinner tonight?"

Elaine seemed to breathe a sigh of relief that they were changing the subject, and she grew excited as she began to rattle off what she had prepared for the night. "I've made fried chicken, mashed potatoes with gravy, green beans, and homemade biscuits. We have homemade Kentucky Derby Pie for dessert."

"Wow. You went all out. I'm going to feel spoiled after this."

The four made their way into the dining room. The room had a simple rectangular layout, but the dining table was eye-catching, polished to a brilliant shine.

"That's a beautiful table," marveled Earl.

"I made it myself in my shop," proclaimed Hank with a hint of pride edging his voice. "It's solid oak. Had a heck of a time getting it into the house … took nearly half a day."

"I'm impressed. Do you sell the things you make?"

"Some. But every piece is quality made. That takes time. I can't make pieces quick enough to have a sufficient inventory to sale in quantity. What I do is more a hobby than a business."

"Tell the Pastor what you've been working on," coaxed Elaine.

"I don't imagine the Pastor is interested in that," Hank replied sheepishly.

Elaine ignored the opinion of her husband and answered for him. "Hank is making a scaled, miniature model of the old Pinewood Church."

"At least you didn't say dollhouse this time," disclosed Hank.

"Well, you've chastised me enough times for calling it that," accused Elaine.

"That's impressive," admitted Earl.

"I've almost finished it. Maybe by Christmas."

Earl caught Harmony sending an apparent facial signal to Elaine. "We need to eat before the food gets cold," declared Elaine.

As they ate, they talked about neutral topics, mostly small talk. Earl was stuffed after the meal. "That was the best meal I've had since I've been back."

Elaine smiled, her face beaming with pride at the compliment.

"What can I do to help clean up?" asked Earl.

"Nothing," exclaimed Elaine. You're a guest. I've got this. We have a fire pit in the back yard, if you and Harmony want to go talk. That will give Hank a chance to watch tv. He likes his alone time, and he hasn't had any today."

Harmony grabbed Earl's coat, and she got hers. Once outside, both Harmony and Earl worked on getting the fire started. After about fifteen minutes, the fire was roaring and shooting flames. Earl and Harmony sat side by side on finished log with a back attached to it that Hank had made.

"I'm sorry about the church talk," winced Harmony. "I honestly didn't think that they would bring it up."

"It was my fault," confessed Earl. "I was searching for something to say, and I asked the wrong question. I knew it was a mistake as the last word came out of my mouth, but it was too late. I couldn't take it back."

"I hope you don't regret coming over."

Earl winked. "Probably not as much as you did when you came over to the parsonage, and I unloaded on you."

"I guess we're even, huh?"

"I guess so."

Both chuckled softly.

"So, what do your parents think of you going to Pinewood Church when they couldn't agree on going to Pinewood Church themselves?"

Harmony appeared deep in thought. "They certainly didn't try to discourage me, and they seem genuinely interested in what goes on at the church. I think they're just glad I'm going somewhere to church."

"Well, I'm glad you're not just going somewhere. I'm glad you chose Pinewood Church." Earl squeezed her hand.

"Me too!"

Harmony leaned against Earl as they sat near the warmth of the fire. The night was clear, and the stars shone brightly, twinkling like fairy lights in Shakespeare's *A Midsummer Night's Dream*. Earl peered into Harmony's eyes. The firelight danced in her eyes like the twinkling stars in the sky. The leaned in with mouth's parted and kissed. Earl's insides felt as though two of the stars in the sky collided, sending a shower of fireworks coursing through his body. When their lips parted, their noses brushed against each other, and Harmony resumed her previous position and leaned back again against Earl. There was nowhere he would rather be than here with

Harmony in this moment. They sat in the silence of each other's company for several minutes.

"What are you doing tomorrow night?" asked Harmony.

"Nothing in particular. Why?"

"I ... never mind."

Earl leaned forward to look into Harmony's face. "You can't start to say something and then say *never mind*."

"What do you mean, *I can't?* I just did." Harmony's mouth cracked a smile.

"You **shouldn't** start to say something and then say *never mind*," quipped Earl.

"There's a Christmas Play tomorrow night in Knoxville. The drive each way is about an hour-and- a-half. I was going to ask if you wanted to go, but we wouldn't get back until midnight or later."

"I'd love to go," beamed Earl. "I'm not going to turn into a pumpkin at midnight."

"You might be as lethargic as a pumpkin the next day though."

"As you advised me the other night. I can always sleep in an extra hour the next day. What time does it start?"

"Seven-thirty."

"Although at the moment, I don't feel as though I need to eat anything for two days, we probably need to eat dinner before it starts. Could you leave at three tomorrow afternoon? That should give us time to get there, eat, and then get to the play in plenty of time."

"Three would be great, if it's not taking you away from anything."

"It's not. I'll pick you up at three." Earl knew he should probably leave, but he didn't want to. "I'll go tell your parents good-bye and thank them again for dinner tonight. I really should be going."

As Earl drove back to the parsonage, he knew he was in love. He just hoped that Harmony felt the same way.

The next afternoon, Earl had just left the parsonage to pick up Harmony for their date to see the Christmas Play in Knoxville when his phone rang. When Earl answered the phone, William's voice came through.

"Hey, Earl, one of my church members went to buy a Christmas Tree last night and said your church had sold out of trees."

"I picked up ten trees this morning from Farmer Brown," replied Earl.

"That's not very many. If you need some help, I've got time this afternoon to help you get some more."

"I appreciate that, but I'm leaving to take Harmony on a date. We're going to watch a Christmas Play in Knoxville. I'll pick up some more trees tomorrow."

"That's wonderful news!" exclaimed William. "You and Harmony make a great couple. I'm excited for you."

"Thanks. I had dinner last night at Harmony's parent's house. I made a mistake of asking where they went to church. They haven't been to church since Pinewood Church split and moved to its current location. The old location meant a lot to Harmony's father. He's making a scaled model of the church. He does wonderful work."

"It sounds like you and Harmony are seeing quite a bit of each other. I'll let you go so that you can get to Knoxville in time, but if you need some help with trees, let me know."

Chapter Eighteen

Earl enjoyed the outing with Harmony. They had dinner at a quaint restaurant in Knoxville before going to see the Christmas Play. As they drove back from the play that got into a conversation about the youth from the mobile home development.

"I haven't been able to stop thinking about what Maria said that night at the pizza parlor," shuddered Harmony. "The bank I'm the branch manager of foreclosed on her family's house."

"You weren't even here at the time. Even if you had been here, what could you have done? If people can't make payments, the bank has little choice."

"That may be true, but it still bothers me."

"I know what you mean. The thought of Luis, or any of them for that matter, having to drop out of school to help their families is a disturbing thought for me. Luis is a smart kid. If he drops out of school, that will just continue the generational poverty for him."

"I wish we could do something to help, but I have no idea what that would be."

"I have an idea. It won't help the foreclosure situation, but it could help with the education piece. I wonder if we could get some folks to help start scholarships for disadvantaged or impoverished youth in Pinewood?"

"That's a great idea!" squealed Harmony. "The bank has a foundation. I'm sure some of the money raised could go to that."

"I imagine some folks in town would make some contributions. We just have to figure out how to market it."

Earl and Harmony continued to talk about how to implement the scholarship idea, but they never settled on a specific action plan.

The drive back seemed to go quickly, but time had gone just as quickly, and Earl didn't make it back to the parsonage until after midnight.

Over the next few days, Earl and Harmony saw each other every day, and Earl couldn't remember feeling happier. He carried this happiness with him almost continually. He was thinking of Harmony as he glided along the sidewalks of Pinewood. Earl was in a happy daydream when the door to the pharmacy opened, almost knocking him down. He was almost floored when he literally bumped into Richard Coldwell, and his daydream quickly evaporated.

"I'm ... sorry." The words stuck in his throat as he came face-to-face with the man who had sent him on a downward spiraling path.

A snarl formed on Richard's face at sight of Earl. One corner of his lip curled upward revealing a couple of teeth. "I heard you were back in town." His voice had lost some of its original strength, but it was raw and still potent. "I can't believe you dared to show back up here. You made a mess of things the last time you were here. This town doesn't need you messing up anymore."

Although Earl wanted to run, he knew he needed to face the personification of his fear. "I'm back to reconcile with my past here." He didn't know if either sentiment or logic would win any points with Richard. "I know we probably won't be friends, but can we be civil toward each other?" Earl had taken the first step toward reconciling with Richard. It was up to him now to decide on the next step.

"There is no reconciliation with us." Richard paused. His eyes looked moist, and he struggled to speak. Earl put two and two together. He had seen Richard coming out of the pharmacy twice now. Had he had a stroke? Worse? Finally, the words came to Richard. "That boy with the rock in his hand. It wasn't him."

Earl was leaning toward stroke or brain tumor. Richard wasn't making any sense to him. "I'm not following."

Richard looked at Earl with scowling eyes. "He wasn't the one who broke the windows. He just happened to come by and pick up a rock that had been dropped. I found out later that my son and some of the other boys in our church broke several of the stained-glass windows." Richard looked down at his feet. He seemed to retreat into himself. He was still a formidable presence, but he seemed damaged now. "We got into an argument, and he left home. I haven't seen him since." Earl could feel the pain in his voice, and he almost felt sorry for the man. That night at the church hadn't just affected Earl, it had affected Richard too. When he had heard Richard left the church, Earl assumed it was because he had ruined it for him. That didn't seem to be true now. "My wife was never the same after that. She died without reconciling with our son. If you would have paid attention to your own flock instead of running around helping those outside of the church, you could have helped our children. You could have prevented that whole string of events from happening."

So now, not only was Earl to blame for ruining the church, he was to blame for Richard's son leaving and for his wife dying. That should be a stretch even for Richard. Earl looked down at the package from the pharmacy in Richard's hand, and Richard noticed Earl spying.

"I've found out that I only have about a year to live. I'll die without ever reconciling with my son too." Richard brushed past Earl and hurried away.

That night, Harmony was at the parsonage, and Earl related the day's events to her. "And then he walked off after dropping that bombshell."

"He wants to blame someone, and you're an easy target. Even if you had devoted all of your attention to those boys in the church, that still might not have prevented what happened."

"Maybe ... maybe not." Earl paused, not knowing whether to share something with Harmony that had been bothering him. But Harmony could read him like a book.

"Something's bothering you. Out with it."

"The last time you said that. Things didn't go well."

"I disagree. If something's bothering you, you need to share it with someone. I know I didn't react well, but I wasn't judging you. I didn't know how to help at the time. I hope you know that I support you even if I don't react the way I should."

Earl figured he would try again. "You asked the other night if I was afraid of Richard. To be honest, I don't know. What I do know is that I was the one who ruined the church. I was the one who kept people from returning to the church. I was the one who made no difference in anyone's lives. I was the one who didn't help the youth in my own church. I was the one whose ego at his ability to serve the community caused everything to come crashing down. My sentence for that is to continually pay penance."

"That not what you preach. That's not what you believe for others. Why do you believe that for yourself?"

"For God to use me, I have to be in a relationship with him. That can't happen without forgiveness."

"I've seen God use people for his purpose who didn't have a relationship with him. Besides, I think you have a better relationship than you are willing to admit."

"I'm lucky to have you."

"Well, I can't argue with you on that note," she teased. "Do you have plans tomorrow?"

"No."

"You do now. I want you to go somewhere with me."

Earl was curious. "Where?"

"Oh no. It's a surprise. You'll find out tomorrow."

Chapter Nineteen

Earl sat quietly as Harmony drove. She had been very secretive. He was somewhat surprised that she had not blindfolded him. When she pulled into the parking lot of Churchdale Barbecue, a pit formed in this stomach that matched the lump in his throat?

"What are we doing here?" Earl could feel the tension in his own voice.

"What do you think? We're going to have lunch."

"I can't go in there."

With simple logic, Harmony explained. "You said the bishop sent you here to come to terms with your past. To do that you're going to have to face some unpleasant things. You can start by going in."

Earl knew she was right. He didn't need to let the place be a painful reminder without at least trying to face his fear. "Alright. As long as you're with me."

Earl felt comforted by Harmony's confident smile. Earl reached out and took Harmony's hand in his. Earl released Harmony's hand temporarily as they got out of the car, but he held it again as they walked toward the restaurant.

"How are all of the stained-glass windows intact? So many were broken, and they look identical to the original ones. Surely the restaurant didn't invest in the windows; they are expensive."

"I don't really know. Honestly. Not all of them were broken, and the ones that were broken were replaced at some point."

"They're beautiful."

Earl faced his trepidation and opened the door. The scent of wood and barbecue that was strong outside, was even stronger inside. Earl stopped at the door and surveyed the inside of the former church. It was decorated for Christmas, and there was a large crowd of people inside. A band was setting up to play.

"Not exactly how you left it, is it?"

Earl was still surveying the restaurant. "No. Parts are still recognizable. They even have some of the pews from the church. They look refurbished." The polished oak shined with new vigor. Now, they were just used as seating for people eating at the restaurant rather than for worship. Seeing them here seemed strange to Earl.

Earl marveled at the beauty and craftsmanship of the new windows and compared them to the original windows that remained intact. To the casual observer, there were hardly any distinguishable differences. The red, orange, yellow, blue, green, and purple colors of the glass each played a cohesive part in casting light into the restaurant. The red, orange, and yellow sections of the glass cast warm, golden flickering hues of flame-like light that helped create a cozy, inviting atmosphere. The blue, green, and purple sections of the glass cast cooler, serene tones.

"There's an empty table over there," called out Harmony over the noise in the restaurant when she spotted the table. "Let's grab it before someone else does."

Harmony rushed to the table, and Earl followed behind. He held the chair for Harmony as she sat down. Earl sat next to her, and they picked up menus from the table.

"So, I hear this is a very popular place. It must be good with as many people as there are here."

"It is. I'm sorry it took you so long to get here."

"Well, by hook or by crook, I'm here now."

A waitress in her early to mid-twenties spotted them and came over. She appeared harried from the crowd of people, but she seemed friendly. "Hi, Harmony."

"Hi, Emily."

Earl caught Emily glance at him. She probably assumed that he was Harmony's boyfriend, just as Samantha Estes had. Then, Emily did a double take and stared intently at Earl. "Pastor Earl?"

"Yes," he replied.

She seemed both excited and a little dishcartened at the same time. "You don't remember me, do you?"

Earl looked her directly in the face. "I'm sorry, but I don't."

"I'm Emily Davis. I was probably around twelve when you pastored the church here."

Earl stroked his chin and thought. "I don't remember a family named Davis in the church. Is Davis your married name?"

"No. I'm not married. I didn't go to church here. I lived in the mobile home park where the housing development now stands."

Excitement showed on Earl's face. "Wait, I do remember you. You were the girl who sprained her ankle."

"And you showed me how to wrap it."

The memory came flooding back to Earl. "That's right!"

"You got me interested in helping people. It's because of you that I'm studying to be a nurse. I'm working here to pay my way through nursing school. I can't believe you're here. I've wanted to thank you for so long, and I finally get to. Thank you. Are you just passing through?"

"I'm pastoring Pinewood Church temporarily until they get a new pastor."

The excitement couldn't be contained on Emily's face. "I'll bring you and Harmony a sampler platter. It's on the house."

"Emily rushed off, ecstasy carrying her on its wings.

Earl had turned to watch Emily as she hurried away, and then he turned back around to face Harmony with joy on his face.

Harmony peered deeply into Earl's eyes. The look captivated him, and he focused solely on her.

"That's your first gift," Harmony exclaimed.

Earl was momentarily taken aback. Gift? Then the letter and note he received sank in, and he was stymied. "What?"

A smile involuntarily erupted over Harmony's face. "Learning about Emily is the first of the three gifts you were promised to receive before Christmas."

Earl was thoroughly perplexed. Knitting his eyebrows together, he asked, "So, you are behind the letter?"

"No," confessed Harmony. "I was just asked to bring you here to get your first gift of seeing the difference you made in someone's life."

Curiosity coursed through Earl's veins. "Well, who's behind the letter?"

Harmony couldn't help but smile at Earl's curiosity. She took both pleasure and sorrow in her response. "I'm sorry, but I've been sworn to secrecy."

More questions had entered Earl's mind than he feared he would receive answers for. "Did Emily know I was coming? She looked surprised to see me."

"No, she didn't know."

Earl spotted Emily and noticed her looking in the direction of the band. When Emily came over to let them know their food would arrive shortly, Earl noticed her glancing toward the band once again. "Do you know someone in the band?" asked Earl.

"Oh, the drummer is my boyfriend."

"Did you just start dating?"

"No. We've been dating a while, but they usually play in Nashville. It's been a while since they've played here. I'm just taking him in while I have the chance."

Suddenly, a stray thought floated through Earl's mind. "Is the owner here, by chance?"

Emily appeared surprised. "You don't have a complaint, do you?"

"Not at all. Just a question that I wanted to ask?"

"He's in back. I'll take you to him."

Harmony narrowed her eyebrows, and Earl could tell she was suspicious of something.

"It's no big deal," reassured Earl. "I'll be back in a jiffy."

"You'd better be. If our food comes while you're gone it will get cold. Nobody wants cold barbeque."

Earl scampered off with Emily leading the way. She took Earl to an enclosed office, and Earl saw the owner sitting behind a desk.

The owner looked to be in his fifties. He was bald in the middle of his head and had patches of grayish hair on the sides. He wore reading glasses as he peered through a ledger. Emily cleared her throat, causing him to look up.

"Mr. Huntley," chirped Emily, this is pastor Earl Stanley of Pinewood Church. He asked to see you." Having made the introduction, Emily quickly absconded from the office.

"Hello, Pastor Stanley. My name is Ron Huntley, but you can call me *Monk*, like everyone else does. It's the hairstyle that earned me that nickname. I became bald on the top of my head by the time I was thirty. People have been calling me Monk ever since. What can I do for you pastor? You haven't come to take the building back for the church, have you?" He stood up, came around the desk, and shook Earl's hand with such vigor that Earl thought his shoulder would come out of its socket.

Monk was a jovial soul, the kind of person that anyone, even a stray dog, would take a liking to. A smile seemed to come easily to his face. The smile, and what seemed to be a permanent squint in his eyes, created crisscrossed wrinkles in the corners of his eyes. Otherwise, his face was as smooth as the bald spot on the top of his head.

Earl took an instant liking to the man, even though he had just met him. He seemed really genuine. "No, I haven't come to take the building back. But I did want to ask you something about the property when you bought it. There was a founder's stone with the names of the families who helped build the old church. I heard it was disposed of, but I thought it wouldn't hurt to ask about it."

"Know exactly what you're talking about," confirmed Monk. "When I bought the place, I asked the preacher then if-in he didn't want it. He said *no.* So, I didn't ask again."

"So, it has been disposed of then," fretted Earl.

"No. I wouldn't go throwing away a piece of history, even if it was just a rock. Something so important that people inscribed their names into stone has to be important to somebody. I still have it. It's in a storage building. I'll be happy to give it to you if you like."

Earl felt fireworks going off inside, although he didn't know why. This place haunted him. He supposed he knew it was important to Harmony's father, and Harmony was important to Earl. "That's wonderful news. I can't take it now, though. Can I call you later about getting it?"

"Sure. It's heavy, and it ain't going nowhere. When you want it, I'll get some people to bring it to you." He winked at Earl. "People who don't know better yet than to go picking up heavy rocks."

"Thank you so much, Monk." Earl absently mindedly stuck out his hand, forgetting the vigor of the previous handshake. He was quickly reminded when his shoulder was jerked a couple of inches lower from the force. Earl turned to leave but quickly spun, wearing a curious expression of scrunched up eyebrows, a lined forehead, and a slightly raised corner of his mouth. "If your name is Huntley, and people call you Monk, why did you name this place Churchdale Barbeque and not Huntley's Barbeque or Monk's Barbeque?"

"Well, I thought it was obvious. And it especially should be obvious to a preacher. This used to be a church, and it's in a dale, like that old song. So that's why I called it Churchdale. You have to have a little vanity to name a place after yourself, and I didn't want to start to go down that road. That's why I don't object to the name, Monk. It keeps me humble."

Earl chuckled and returned to his table. Emily had just set the food on the table, and he had arrived just in time to avoid a scolding eye from Harmony.

"What did you talk to the owner about?" quizzed Harmony, still wearing the puzzled expression on her face.

Earl grinned from ear to ear. "I can't let you be the only one of us with a secret. Now eat up before it gets cold. Nobody wants cold barbeque."

After eating at Churchdale, Harmony and Earl headed back to town.

"What did you think of the food?" inquired Harmony.

Earl rubbed his belly. "It's as good as everyone said. I'm stuffed. I don't think I need to eat dinner tonight. The sampler platter was huge, pulled pork, sausage, ribs, corn, beans, bread, and I'm sure I'm forgetting something. I think maybe Emily gave us more than what she was supposed to."

"What did you think of your first gift?"

"I'm glad if I inspired Emily. I'm really thankful for the gift. But it still doesn't outweigh my neglect of the congregation. It doesn't outweigh the tearing apart of a church. It doesn't outweigh the fact that people turned away from the church. As you said, it wasn't just Pinewood Church that they turned away from; they're no longer going to any church. I'm afraid it's going to take more than that for me to regain my confidence."

"The person behind the gifts must have anticipated that, which is probably why they think it will take three gifts."

"I don't know that there is ever enough I can do to make up for the harm I caused."

Harmony quickly glanced at Earl and just as quickly returned her attention to driving. Harmony slowed down as the car approached a bare spot alongside the road that looked like it had been used as a roadside pull out. Harmony pulled in and put the car in park. She turned in her seat to face Earl. "I don't believe what my ears are hearing. You're a gifted minister, schooled in a seminary. It never occurred to me that you don't believe what you preach!" Harmony shook her head. Her face reddened with anger. "You know God's forgiveness is bigger than any one event. Don't you preach that God will forgive you no matter what you've done if you repent?" Harmony blew a frustrated breath from her mouth. She bowed her head as if in prayer, and then pulled the car back onto the road.

Earl was taken aback by Harmony's outburst. He had not seen her this fired up. "Of course, you're right." Earl didn't want to go down the road that he had with Harmony the night they decorated the tree. He didn't want to create a persona of *poor, pitiful me*. He knew he needed to change the subject. "Jarrett Bridges is arriving the day after tomorrow with the shoes, basketball goals, and backboards. I'm glad the youth will have everything before

Christmas. I'm going to help ... well at least show him where the mobile home neighborhood is. He's got some people to help replace the goals. Do you want to come with me?"

"Sure! That would be great."

Apparently, Harmony was quick to forgive, and he was certainly glad of that. "I'll pick you up around lunchtime."

The next day, Earl was in the Pinewood Church Study working on Sunday's sermon when he heard a knock on the doorframe. Earl looked up from his notes and saw Ted Long standing at the door with his arms crossed and a sour expression on his face. Earl quickly glanced at his watch. The time was five thirty-five. No wonder Ted looked cross. The church sold Christmas Trees from five o'clock until eight o'clock every day except Sunday. Tonight was Earl's turn to man the tree sale, and he had completely forgotten about it. "Ted, I completely forgot the time. I'm going out now."

Earl rushed outside to find several people wanting to buy trees. When he looked for the inventory of trees, he saw none available.

Ted caught up to Earl and stood by his side. "Earl, we have people wanting to buy trees and there are none here. Jerry got a call from Farmer Brown who said he never received another order from you. He expected a call and had cut several trees that have now gone to waste, and he's upset. He could have sold them himself, but he was trying to do us a favor. Remember that the Church Council said that you would have to keep a close eye on the trees. We can't afford to lose that partnership for the future."

"You're right, Ted. I'm sorry. I'll make up for it."

"See that you do." Ted turned and walked toward his car.

Earl walked over and apologized to the people who had come out to buy trees. He asked them to check back tomorrow, and they should have some. Now, Earl needed to figure out how to transport the trees. Jarrett Bridges was coming tomorrow; so, he wouldn't be able to get help from the youth. As long as he could use Jerry's truck and trailer, he would just have to lug them to and from the trailer and set them up himself. Jarrett wouldn't arrive until around noon or one o'clock. He would have to get up early to get the trees.

Earl called Jerry first to make sure he could use the truck and trailer. Jerry volunteered to drive, but his back hurt, and he didn't want to lift or carry any trees. Jerry reiterated that Farmer Brown was upset at not receiving a call and at the loss of good Christmas Trees that took years to grow to that size. Next, Earl called Farmer Brown and apologized profusely. Farmer Brown indicated that he would have to raise the price slightly to the church to make up for the loss. He was also upset that Earl hadn't given him more notice if he expected to pick up trees in the morning. He indicated to Earl that he would only have about twenty trees available on such short notice. Earl told him that was fine. In his mind, Earl thought that twenty trees were plenty, especially if he were loading and unloading them himself. He was also reminded of Ted Long's charge to not have many trees left over. Now that Farmer Brown was going to raise the price slightly, Earl would have to doubly make sure that no trees went unsold.

Chapter Twenty

The next morning, Earl and Jerry left at seven in the morning to head to the farm. When they arrived, Farmer Brown, dressed in blue overhauls, was just beginning to cut trees. Farmer Brown was surprised that Earl didn't have more help. Although Earl agreed, he thought to himself that would be true if the trees were already cut, but he didn't see the point in having a lot of people to carry one tree every few minutes.

Earl carried each tree as it was cut to the trailer. The morning was warmer than usual, and soon sweat trickled down his cheeks. Earl regretted that he had not brought another shirt along. The one he was wearing would have been perfect if the weather was twenty degrees colder, but it was entirely too warm for this weather.

Earl also wondered if it had been a mistake to bring Jerry along. After every tree that was cut, Farmer Brown and Jerry would talk about umpteen different topics, like two old men sitting in chairs at the country store or barber shop with nothing else to do. He wished that he could have come by himself. Of course, he was not used to driving a truck with a trailer attached, and he wouldn't have felt comfortable driving someone else's vehicle anyway.

After a few hours, the last tree was loaded. But then Jerry performed an inspection and ordered Earl to adjust the load. Then he provided specific instructions on how to tie down the trees and what knots to use, which Jerry instructed Earl how to tie, why that particular knot was used, and the history of the knot.

When they were finally ready to leave, Earl was so hot, he was lightheaded. He swore to himself that if he closed his eyes, someone could have told him it was the middle of July, and he would have believed them. Earl was just about to ask Jerry about lowering the passenger door window, but Jerry turned up the heat.

Arriving at the church, Earl hurriedly unloaded the trees. Jerry was beginning to tell him how to set up the trees, but Earl told him he would take care of it that night; he needed to get cleaned up and get to the mobile home neighborhood. Jerry just shook his head at Earl's decision, but fortunately he didn't say anything.

Once Jerry left, Earl went directly to the parsonage, chugged two tall glasses of water, stripped, and stood in a cold shower. He dressed in something that wouldn't be as warm. It was five minutes to noon when Earl left to go pick up Harmony at the bank. He hoped that Jarrett wouldn't arrive for another hour.

Earl and Harmony arrived at the mobile home park basketball court around twelve thirty. Jarrett had not arrived yet, but the group of teens were gathered in anticipation, displaying nervous energy. Some clowned around. Others started a quick game of basketball while they waited. The sounds of shoes scuffing against the asphalt, the bouncing ball, the thud of a ball against the old backboards, and the lively banter and laughter energized Earl. Soreness had already begun to set in, but the energy around him somehow made him feel younger, much younger than he had around Jerry and Farmer Brown. Earl counted a total of twenty teens. Four more teens had somehow magically appeared from the number he had given Jarrett.

At one o' clock on the dot., the sound of a vehicle approaching caused everyone to stop what they were doing. Only the sound of the vehicle's engine could be heard. A long black limousine came into sight, and suddenly, a ripple of excitement spread like a wildfire through the assembled group as all eyes were on the limo. Pulling up the rear was a truck.

Jarrett is pulling out all the stops, thought Earl.

"Is it really him?" someone asked in a hushed voice.

The limo came to a stop, and the crowd buzzed with excitement and anticipation. Out of the limo stepped a tall, instantly recognizable figure dressed in his team uniform.

"Earl, my man. It's good to see you. Get ready. Once everything is set up, I'm challenging you to a game! And I brought you a new pair of shoes so that you have no excuse when you go down."

A smile instantly formed on Earl's face, bringing forth a loud laugh. It was kind of Jarrett to acknowledge Earl first. Earl knew that Jarrett did that for the explicit purpose of cementing Earl's position with the youth.

Phones were whipped out to capture the moment, and the group rushed to Jarrett, but Luis called out in a commanding voice, "Ok, everybody, give Mr. Bridges some space." Everyone stopped short of Jarrett.

Jarrett was smiling and laughing, clearly in his element. He slapped hands, high-fived, and fist-bumped every person gathered around him. Jarrett reached into the limo and pulled out a large box filled with basketball jerseys. He called out sizes and tossed them as people raised their hands. Four people from the truck carried boxes of shoes. Jarrett had apparently anticipated that more than sixteen pairs of shoes would be needed; he had more than enough. He autographed them personally before handing them out, and he even gave pairs to Earl and Harmony.

With the jerseys and shoes distributed, the work crew began work on replacing the backboards. Jarrett strode to the court dribbling a basketball, and the youth gathered around him, mouths agape. Jarrett posed for selfies with each person.

As the old backboards were quickly dismantled and new ones mounted, Jarrett passed out brand new basketballs from a box a worker set near him. The sound of bouncing balls and the smell of new shoes and basketballs filled the air. Next, new nets were installed.

Jarrett performed a few slam dunks and put on a dribbling exhibition before offering tips. The youth soaked it all in. Noisy chatter erupted when Jarrett asked to form teams. He alternated playing on different teams and played on a team with each of the teens there. Harmony and Earl played too, and everyone watched with rapt attention when Earl and Jarrett played half-court one-on-one.

Jarrett stayed until darkness crept in. Before leaving, he took a moment to speak to them. "I'll come back in January and give you some more pointers. You guys listen to Pastor Earl. He may not be able to play basketball, but he's a good guy, and he sure can preach.

Several of his sermons have stuck with me. If any of you ever go through a difficult time, this man will help you."

The youth hung on every word and waved good-bye as he walked back to the limo. Earl went with him. "Thanks for coming, Jarrett. I owe you."

"You don't owe me anything. I'm happy to help. If a couple of small things from me can help turn some teens' lives around, I'm happy to do it. Any time you need something from me, just let me know. And you have a great girlfriend there. Don't lose the ball."

"Not if I can help it." Everyone Earl and Harmony met seemed to think they were an item. Perhaps they suited each other well. Earl thought so, and he definitely didn't want to lose the ball where Harmony was concerned.

As Earl and Harmony were getting into Earl's car to leave, Luis ran over.

"Pastor. Thank you for what you did. Nobody's done anything like that for us before. You understand we were skeptical. I don't understand you, but I appreciate what you've done."

As they drove off, Harmony commented, "That was a great thing you did for them. See. You're still making a difference in people's lives."

"It wasn't me. If it weren't for Jarrett, none of this would have happened."

"Without you, none of this would have happened."

Earl smiled. He was too tired to argue. Besides, he felt good.

Harmony continued. "Maybe you're starting to learn one of your lessons of letting others help. Thanks for inviting me. That was fun. I haven't played basketball in a while. I'll probably be sore tomorrow."

"Speaking of tomorrow ... tomorrow night, Victorious Life Church is having their Christmas Carnival. Before we left, I invited the youth. I'm interested to see if they come. It's mostly for kids and youth, but would you like to go?

"Sure. You're spoiling me by taking me to so many places."

"Spoiling you by taking you to Farmer Brown's, a barbeque restaurant, the Mainstreet Diner, and a Christmas Carnival? And those are the more outstanding places. Hopefully I'll have a chance to take you out in a larger city."

"I look forward to that."

Earl dropped Harmony off and headed straight for the parsonage. He was going to take another shower when he got back, but he was so tired that he fell onto the bed, fully dressed, and almost immediately went to sleep.

Chapter Twenty-One

A carnival-like atmosphere exuded from the grounds of Victorious Life Church for its festive Christmas Carnival. String lights hung from the overhanging roof of the church with more lights decorating the trees and shrubs. The church also used some of the larger commercial outdoor displays, mostly religious-themed.

The crisp night air was perfect for the Christmas Carnival, and it was filled with the joyful sounds of carolers singing, children laughing, and the steady hum of conversations. It was like a scene from a holiday movie about Christmas in a small town. Earl and Harmony strolled the area taking in the sights, sounds, and smells. A lot was packed into the space.

The first thing they saw was a Ferris Wheel, which was surprising to have for a church Christmas Carnival. They went immediately to that. They had arrived early and barely had to wait until it was their turn to ride. Earl held Harmony's hand as the big wheel lunged upward. Just like in a movie, the Ferris Wheel stopped with Earl and Harmony at the top as some people were let off and others were let on. The view of the decorated grounds below was spectacular. The wheel suddenly lurched forward again, startling Harmony and she clung tightly to Earl's hand. The ride ended too soon for Earl. He enjoyed being alone with Harmony while still being able to enjoy the festivities. The only other ride was a Merry-Go-Round for children. The ride used real ponies supplied by Farmer Brown. Some of the kids beamed with excitement. Others were hesitant and held their parents' hands as the parents walked the circular track beside their children.

Next, Earl and Harmony came to the game section. One of the games was a basketball game, and they saw Luis trying out some of the shooting skills that Jarrett showed. Luis hit five shots in a row and won a basketball as a prize.

"Nice shooting, Luis," called Earl. "I'm glad to see that you came tonight. It looks like Jarrett's visit paid off."

"Hi, Pastor Earl. The shoes are great. They helped us all play better, and the new goals are awesome. Thanks again for setting all that up."

"You're a shrewd negotiator, Luis. If you need a career besides basketball, I can think of several that would make use of your negotiating skills. Next time I need to buy a car, I'm bringing you with me!"

Earl and Harmony played a few games. One was a ring toss game, but neither did very well. Next was tossing marshmallows into mugs of hot chocolate. Harmony did pretty well but not well enough to win a prize. Earl decided he would fare better simply eating his marshmallows. He took one bite and had to forcefully swallow the mouthful of marshmallow. They were so stale, he wondered if they had been left over from last year. The final game they played was another tossing game. This game had sixteen-ounce plastic cups laid out in the shape of a Christmas tree. All but four of the cups were green. Of the four cups that weren't green, three cups were red, and one was blue. The object of the game was to toss a ping pong ball into one of the four specially colored cups. Both

Earl and Harmony tossed a ping pong ball into a cup, but it was a green cup. So, neither of them won a prize.

Harmony wanted to go to the crafts section; so, they headed there next. Some people were selling quilts, needlepoint designs, scarves, mittens, and so forth. Another section had long tables covered with red and green tablecloths that were laden with supplies for making ornaments, wreaths or for decorating cookies. Jerry was trying his hand at piping icing onto cupcakes. He had three cupcakes with globs of icing, and he was concentrating hard on perfecting the fourth; his tongue stuck out from his effort at concentrating. Another area in the craft section was dedicated to designing ugly Christmas sweaters. Neither Earl nor Harmony brought a sweater; so, they just looked on. William was decorating a sweater, but Earl wouldn't call the design ugly. If fact, it was beautiful. He didn't know William was such an artist.

A quartet of carolers dressed in Victorian costumes sang Christmas Carols next to the food and beverage section. The four-part harmony of traditional carols floated through the air attracting a large crowd. Many sang along. Although the previous church Earl pastored performed more contemporary music, there was something about the old nostalgic carols that uplifted the heart.

Nearby was a firepit where families huddled together roasting marshmallows on long sticks above the dancing flames. The scents of roasted marshmallows mingled with nearby tantalizing scents of cotton candy, freshly popped popcorn, mulled apple cider, and hot chocolate were a treat to the nose.

"Would you like a cup of hot chocolate?" asked Earl. Harmony was quiet, apparently absorbed in thought, and Earl repeated the question. "Would you like a cup of hot chocolate?"

"What? ... Oh ... Yes. That would be great."

Earl ordered two hot chocolates. He called back to Harmony. "Would you like marshmallows or whipped cream?" Harmony didn't reply, and Earl asked for both marshmallows and whipped cream in each. He paid for the drinks and carried them carefully so as to not spill the hot liquid on his hands. "Be careful. It's hot." He handed one to Harmony. "You seem a million miles away tonight. Is something bothering you?"

Harmony peered up at Earl with wide eyes, wide enough that Earl could see the concern in them. "Can we go somewhere sort of private and talk?" she asked.

"Sure." Now, Earl was concerned. He took Harmony to the reflection garden. Fortunately, no one else was there, but the muffled sounds of the carnival drifted over to their private sanctuary. They sat on a bench that was stone-cold from the night air.

They sat in silence for several seconds. When it became apparent to Earl that Harmony was having a difficult time telling him whatever it was that she wanted him to hear, he finally asked. "What's up?"

Harmony's eyes were tuned to the ground. "I got a job offer today at a bank in Philadelphia. It's a vice president job like I wanted." Her voice was marked by palpable hesitation. "I'm going to take it."

The words hit Earl like a truck from out of nowhere. He knew he needed to be supportive even if he didn't want to. Not really knowing what to say, he went with a basic investigative question. "When does it start?"

"I need to leave as soon as possible."

The truck that hit Earl had backed up and run over him again. "Wow," he replied with the weakest of enthusiasm. "Well, I'm happy for you." It wasn't true, but what else could he say? He was quiet, lost in his own thoughts and wondering what to say.

"Is that all you have to say?" Harmony's voice seemed to beg for something, but Earl wasn't sure what that was.

He finally decided to be honest, to risk being hurt. "What can I say? I want you to stay. I thought there was something between us, but I can't let you sacrifice that for me."

Tears began to well in Harmony's eyes, but they held fast. Harmony's voice cracked as she spoke. "There is something between us, and I know it can grow into a lot more, but you'll be leaving here yourself soon to who knows where. We can still try to make it work."

Earl felt he should have realized that his relationship with Harmony had been too good to be true. Pinewood never disappointed in beating him down. "Long-distance relationships don't work. Even if you have weekends off, that's when I'll be preaching. And I'm supposed to be in Dallas, Texas in July. Dallas and Philadelphia are so far apart; I don't see any way a relationship can work."

A hint of indignation invaded Harmony's voice. "So, we're just going to give up on it?"

Earl wondered what answer Harmony was looking for from him. "What else can we do? We'll both be so busy, especially in new jobs, that we'll hardly ever have time to talk to each other, much less see each other. You mean a lot to me. You're the bright spot of my time here. I don't want to be without you, but I don't know of any alternatives."

"I guess you're right."

Despite her statement, Earl felt she believed he was anything but right. They both sat quietly for a few minutes. Then, as if spurred by the same thought, both rose. Harmony grabbed Earl, pulling him to her. She kissed him passionately, as if it were their first, last, and only kiss.

"I love you!" she affirmed; then she turned and ran off.

"I love you too, Harmony." But only the dark night was witness to his attestation.

Chapter Twenty-Two

Earl was back on par with his sermons. Even so, his mind was occupied with thoughts of Harmony. Fortunately, for Earl those thoughts didn't affect his sermon. After the Sunday worship service, as the parishioners exited, Ted Long was the last to leave. Ted's face exhibited the stern look that seemed to be the hallmark for lead laypersons of Pinewood Church.

"The Church Council wants to meet with you tomorrow night at seven o'clock." Ted dropped the bombshell and huffed off, leaving Earl standing by himself in the sanctuary.

Earl smacked himself in the forehead. "I didn't keep in touch with Farmer Brown."

About two o'clock in the afternoon, Earl sat outside on the top step leading up to the parsonage feeling sorry for himself when Harmony drove up and parked. His heart sank when he saw the car loaded down with her belongings. Earl's legs were noodles and gravity pulled hard on him. The combination of effects kept him from being able to move. Harmony got out of her car and shuffled over to Earl and sat beside him.

"Isn't it a little cold to be sitting outside?"

Depression laced his voice. "A little. I'm just reflecting. It looks like you're all packed up. Are you headed out of town?"

"Yes. I'm afraid so. I didn't want to leave everything the way we left it after the carnival. I really do love you. Isn't there some way we can make this work?"

Earl yearned for a solution. He had thought of multiple potential solutions, but each one seemed to fall short. Harmony had asked though if there was some way. It couldn't hurt to offer one. He'd be no worse off than he already was if she didn't like his option. He remembered her previous remark, and he thought, *All she can say is no*. "You could stay here, and I could request to stay at the church."

Harmony stared into the distance. Earl didn't really think she was focusing on anything in particular. She waited a few seconds before replying. "I don't mind compromising, but both of us giving up our dreams is not going to work. It's not fair for either of us."

Earl tried another of his ideas. "You could come to Dallas."

Harmony guffawed. "As what, your girlfriend? Then I'd be without a job to afford a place to stay. That won't go over well with your church either. They'd think I was a tag-along mistress."

"We could get married."

"I don't want to get married to solve a problem. Call me old fashioned, but I want to marry for love."

"I do love you."

"I love you too, Earl, and I hope you find peace. If you had the confidence that you had when you were here twelve years ago, you'd be unstoppable."

Without warning, Harmony hopped up and hurried to her car. Within one minute, she was out of sight and out of Earl's life.

Monday night arrived, and the last place Earl wanted to be was facing the Church Council. Harmony leaving hit him hard. It was all he had thought about since her departure. She was gone in a flash. No kiss. No lingering good-bye. No looking back; she had certainly paid attention to the lesson of Sodom and Gomorrah about not looking back. Earl had not even prepared an explanation or response to the questions he knew the Church Council would ask.

Earl waited outside of the meeting room until he was called in. He took his place, standing in front of the council members like an accused criminal. Earl didn't feel anything at first. The first indication that something was coming over him was his breathing. He breathed short, erratic breaths, causing light-headedness, which ushered in the panic. Suddenly, he felt like he had been transported in time and space.

> Earl was in the meeting room at the old Pinewood Church nearly eleven years ago. He stood before seven church council members who all looked displeased.

> "You were sent here to serve this church," spat Richard, "not spend all of your time running around town, especially not spending so much time at that trailer park helping people who don't even go to church here."

> "But it's the Christian thing to do," answered Earl.

"We pay you to serve our congregation, and
that's what you'll do, or we'll find someone who
will."

The voice of Ted Long shook Earl back to the present, back to
the meeting room in the current Pinewood Church. "Pastor
Stanley," began Ted. "When we were informed that you would
temporarily serve as our pastor, we appreciated your willingness to
come here and serve after the death of our former pastor. We
recognized that it must have been difficult to come back here after
the manner in which you and our church parted company all those
years ago. You have successfully pastored other churches since that
time and have been recognized nationally as an exceptional
preacher. We assumed you had grown as a complete pastor during
that time. However, we've seen you make the same mistakes as you
did when you first served our church. You tend to involve neither
the church congregation nor council in your dealings."

Earl felt like a chastised child, and he had had enough. Before
Ted could continue, Earl interrupted. Defensiveness suffused Earl's
voice. "I was thrown right in the middle of something that most
pastors would have had sufficient time to prepare for. Plus, I've
received practically no help from the congregation."

Ted grew more animated at Earl's outburst. "We urged you to
pay attention to the number of trees we were selling. Farmer Brown
has lost trees that he was practically giving to us because we did not
order enough, and people have come to buy trees only to find an
empty lot."

Earl was fuming. "As far as consulting the Council, the advice you gave was hardly helpful: don't order too many trees but don't order to few either."

Ted's face was red, and anger temporarily tongue-tied him. When he found his voice, it was harsh and unyielding. "The bottom line, Pastor Stanley, is that we have raised nowhere near the money we have in the past. It might be time for us to simply recognize that we are just not a good fit for each other."

"I see. Thank you for your candidness." And with that, Earl stormed out of the room.

Chapter Twenty-Three

On Tuesday afternoon, Earl stuffed the last bag into his car. Placing both hands on his lower back he tried to stretch the tension out. He wasn't sure what he would do with his life or how his actions would fare with the bishop. All he knew was he needed to leave Pinewood.

Jerry ambled up as Earl was stretching. A frown creased his forehead, and he breathed a sigh. "I wish you wouldn't leave, Pastor. It's only nine days to Christmas. Can't you at least stay until then?"

Earl sighed resignedly, and a cloud of humiliation covered his face. "I lost my composure and was defensive with the Church Council. They won't let me stay, and I don't blame them. The whole episode took me back to being in front of the Church Council during Richard Coldwell's tenure, and I didn't want to be bullied anymore."

"I know Richard, and I know Ted. Ted is not a bully. You challenged Ted's authority in front of the other councilmembers. It upset Ted, and he said something he didn't really mean. That doesn't mean they're kicking you out."

"Doesn't it? He can't let such a challenge go … unchallenged, so to speak. I appreciate all you've done Jerry, but I think it's best if I do leave. Take care. I consider you a true friend."

Jerry stared off into nothingness and gave a small nod. He stuck out his hand, and Earl did likewise. Earl squeezed his hand, and Jerry wished him well. "Godspeed, my friend. Godspeed."

The corner of Earl's eyes, and the corners of Earl's mouth lifted in slight smiles. He climbed into the car and drove off.

Before Earl was out of sight, Jerry pulled out his phone and made a call.

Earl was not even two miles from the parsonage when his phone rang. "Hello," he answered.

"Pastor Earl? This is Emily. I really need for you to come by Churchdale Barbecue."

Earl rolled his eyes and just shook his head. Why couldn't he shed this town from him? He felt like he was in an episode of the Twilight Zone. Either that or in one of those dreams where no matter how hard you tried, something always came up to prevent you from getting to your destination. There was a little edginess in his voice as he answered. "Hi, Emily. This is really not a good time."

"It's extremely important. Please come by. I have to see you. It's urgent."

Earl sighed. If he was the type of person to curse, now would be a perfect time for it. He hesitated and could hear Emily's frantic breathing coming through the car speakers. He reconsidered his stance on cursing, but merely shook his head again. "Ok, Emily. I'll be there shortly." He disconnected the call and sighed deeply. "Of all places, why here and why now?" The irony of this situation didn't escape Earl. Around eleven years ago, he was driven from the old Pinewood Church. Now, years later, he was headed back to the same location as his last stop before leaving Pinewood Church once again."

When Earl pulled into the parking lot, he was a little surprised at the number of cars in the parking lot at this time on a Tuesday afternoon. The savory aroma of the cooked pork, chicken, and beef immediately greeted his nose. And he heard the sounds of a band warming up. That was why the parking lot was already crowded; people were here to hear the band.

Emily was near the door waiting for him as he slinked in. He was in a hurry, and he purposed in his mind that he wouldn't let Emily detain him longer than necessary. "Hi, Emily. Look, I'm in a hurry. What's so important?" Earl was in a hurry, but he didn't need to be rude to the young woman. He was sorry for the tone he had used with Emily, but from the look on her face, she didn't seem to have taken any offense to it.

"You can't leave yet."

Earl wondered how she knew he was leaving. Did she mean the restaurant or the town? He assumed she somehow knew he was leaving Pinewood. He didn't want to use an ill tone with her, but maybe he could justify his decision, appeal to her rationale side. "During both of my times here, two different lead laypersons have told me I've failed Pinewood Church. I'm sorry, Emily, but I'm leaving."

Earl was curious about the expression on her face. Her eyes were wide, and she gave quick wandering looks. She was like a rabbit caught between two foxes. Her hands involuntarily smoothed the wrinkles from her uniform in long nervous strokes. She stole a quick glance at the band who had just completed their final checks.

Curiosity transformed into concern. "Is someone bothering you, Emily?"

"What? … Oh, no … nothing like that at all."

That was all Earl needed to hear. He turned and headed for the door. As soon as he put his hand on the door handle, the sound of an acoustic guitar stung his ears with its discordance. The first few chords sounded as if someone was just learning how to play. He felt sorry for the musician. But something seemed vaguely familiar in the chords. He stopped, his hand still on the door handle. A few more strained chords painfully emanated from the guitar. Then, the guitar seemed to awaken; its wooden body resonated with a newfound clarity. The once uncooperative guitar found new life as the strings now danced at a master's touch who, with a gentle caress, coaxed the guitar as it sang a heartfelt and haunting melody, pouring out its emotion and weaving a tapestry of sounds like a master storyteller. Earl recognized the tune. It was an old hymn, *Come to the Church in the Wildwood*, but it wasn't played at its usual quicker pace. It was a slow soulful version. The guitar player began to sing along with his instrument, and a woman in the band harmonized with the slow acoustic version. He had never heard the song played and sung this way. The music called to Earl and gently pulled him from the door to face the band. He, and the entire crowd of people in the restaurant, were mesmerized. The guitar's soul, and the haunting interpretation of the song, touched Earl's own soul. Earl struggled to contain his emotion, but the tears escaped, nonetheless.

The song finished to a hushed silence from the crowd, but the silence lasted only an instant before the crowd erupted into applause.

The guitar player and singer appeared to be in his mid-twenties. "Most of you know my name is Jeff Beckett, but most of you don't know this about me. When I was a boy and in my teens, I lived in the mobile home park where the housing development is near here. My family was poor and could only afford second-hand clothes for me. I was on the rambunctious side, to put it mildly. But a young pastor defied all logic and ministered to everyone there, expecting nothing in return. That pastor gave me this very acoustic guitar I just played. He taught me a few chords and then this song, which was the first song I ever played. If it weren't for him, I wouldn't be where I am today. Merry Christmas, Pastor."

Jeff had addressed Earl, and the crowd in the restaurant turned toward Earl offering applause.

Emily, no longer appearing anxious, smiled at Earl. "That's your second gift, Pastor."

Earl was shaken from his surprise to a newfound surprise. His mouth was agape as he peered into Emily's face. "What? ... Are you the one behind the gifts?"

"No, but I got a call telling me you were leaving. I had to get you to stop here."

"Jerry was the only person who knew the exact time I left. Was it Jerry who called? Is he the one behind the gifts?"

"Jerry was the one who called. I don't know if he is behind the gifts or not. I was only told that I had to get you here at any cost. It was luck that the band was here."

Although the band had played only one song, they took a break. Jeff and several members of the band came over to Emily and Earl. "Let's go outside," urged Jeff, "so that we can talk."

The group found a quiet place outside behind the restaurant, and Jeff began to share his story. "When Emily told me that I was to sing *Come to the Church in the Wildwood*, I jumped at the chance. I've always wanted to show you what you've meant to me. I just didn't know when we were going to play it for you. We were here the other week when you came in, but Emily was the first gift. The restaurant doesn't usually have music on Tuesdays, and we weren't scheduled to play until Thursday, but this close to Christmas, the owner wanted to have live music."

Emily grabbed a member of the band and drug him over to meet Earl. He was reluctant and looked at the ground. "Pastor, I want to introduce you to my boyfriend, Keith. He's the drummer in the band."

Keith reluctantly looked up and, with hesitation, offered his hand to Earl. Earl vigorously shook Keith's hand. "Pastor," said Keith. "I'm Keith Coldwell."

The name escaped Earl's notice at first, but then it came around again and slammed into Earl's head. "Keith ... Coldwell! Richard Coldwell's son?"

Keith hung his head once more and mumbled, "Yes."

"Does your father know you're here?"

Keith's head shot up. "No, and he can't. I was a disappointment to my parents. I was the one who led a group of boys to break some of the stained-glass windows in the church. My parents and I got into a bad argument, and I left. I haven't seen my parents since. I wasn't even at my mother's funeral. I just don't have the courage to face my father."

Earl's heart went out to Keith. It was as though Earl was looking into an emotional mirror. Keith was an emotional reflection of Earl. Richard had emotionally ruined two men. "How can he not know you're here? Surely, someone has recognized you."

"I don't go by Coldwell when Jeff introduces the band. As a drummer, I'm also in the back. Plus, people in town don't expect to see me. It's like hiding in plain sight."

"I met Keith in Nashville," interjected Jeff. "I was playing on the street for money, and Keith was homeless. We didn't run in the same circles, for obvious reasons, here in Pinewood. I was rash to most people in town. Keith was the entitled son of one of the town's wealthiest and most prominent citizens. Still, I recognized him and took him to my run-down apartment. I made him take a shower, first thing. I took him to the barbershop to get a haircut and his beard trimmed. I found out he had been a drummer in several bands, but they would always kick him out."

"I was in a bad place then. If it weren't for Jeff, I don't know what would have become of me."

"We gradually put a band together and started gaining popularity. Things are looking good for us."

"How did you start playing here?" questioned Earl.

Jeff answered. "Emily saw us play in Nashville. She knew me, of course, from the mobile home development, but she didn't know Keith. When the owner of Churchdale Barbeque planned a visit to Nashville, Emily told him to check us out. He saw us play in Nashville and asked if we would come play here. Keith didn't want to come back, but the owner wouldn't take *no* for an answer. We thought we would give it a try."

"They play here whenever they can," exclaimed Emily.

"That's because I got to know Emily and fell in love." Keith reached for Emily's hand and intertwined her fingers in his."

Emily smiled broadly, and Earl could see the young love in both of their faces. "When they're not playing here, they're playing higher paying and more popular gigs."

Earl didn't know exactly what Keith felt towards his father, but he had a pretty good idea. He thought Keith loved his father but that the hurt and pain he had caused his family wouldn't let him go to his father. Earl struggled with what to tell Keith. He didn't know how Richard would react to seeing him. From what Richard told him, he knew that Richard would probably welcome him with open arms, but he couldn't know that for certain. Was it right to keep the news of Richard's illness from Keith? Richard could die, and then, Keith would have lost out not only on seeing his mother but his father as well. The death of Keith's mother and him not attending her funeral had to weigh heavy on Keith. Was it worth the risk to have pain now, to face possible rejection, to go see his father while he still could? If he missed this chance, what would it do to Keith emotionally? A voice inside of Earl told him it was not his right for him to make Keith's decision for him. The voice was right, and Earl blurted out, "Keith, you have to go see your father."

Pain wrenched Keith's face, contorting its otherwise handsome features. "I can't," he managed to eke out. "I've hurt him too badly. He doesn't want to see me."

Earl recognized the emotion that overrode Keith's reasoning abilities. He had to somehow get through that emotion and convince him. "He's dying, and he only has about a year to live. I know I'm not one to talk. I was literally running away, and I'm far from peace myself. It's hard to confront people you feel you've wronged or let down, but it's hard to live with an emotional burden pulling you down. I know, and I know you know that too."

Tears welled in Keith's eyes despite the toughened exterior he had built for himself. Earl could see Keith wrestling with what to do and with the words to say. "What if he doesn't want to see me?"

"I believe he does."

"You believe he does. You're not certain then."

Earl couldn't give Keith the certainty he wanted. That was where faith came in, but Keith had not had the tools to build that faith. "I'm not one hundred percent certain, no. But will that hurt you any more than you've already been hurt? Ask yourself what the consequences are of not going to see him."

Keith's eyes darted between two unseen debaters. The image of a rabbit caught between two foxes came to Earl's mind again. He imagined that Keith wanted to flee to anywhere but here. But Keith surprised him. "I'll try. Will you come with me? And you too, Emily?"

Earl put a sympathetic hand on Keith's shoulder. "I will."

"Of course," echoed Emily.

"What about playing? We have to play here tonight, and Emily has to work."

"I'm sure the owner will let me off," replied Emily.

"Don't worry about the band," insisted Jeff. We've got several songs we can play, and I saw a drummer from another band inside. I can probably convince him to play, if necessary."

Keith looked worried as he shot a wide-eyed glance at Jeff.

"Don't worry," chuckled Jeff. "There's no way we're going to replace you! Now, go!"

Earl retreated back to Pinewood as he drove Keith and Emily to Richard's house. He had to use Emily's car since his car was full to the brim with all of his belongings. Keith sat in the back with

Emily; he was quiet, holding Emily's hand and staring straight ahead. He looked as though he were on his way to an execution.

Richard lived in a well-to-do neighborhood in a large ornate house. The houses were brick with large garages and perfectly manicured lawns. Even at this time of the year, the grass was green. Most of the houses were decorated elaborately for Christmas, and one could see the Christmas Trees displayed through large bay windows. Most of them looked identical with clear lights and the same style of ornaments, as if they had been professionally designed by the same decorator. There was nothing tacky about these trees. Richard's house stood out by its lack of decorations. Emily begged Earl to park along the street. Even though her car was not leaking any fluids, she didn't want to risk blotching the brilliantly white driveway. Earl imagined a wayward elf sneaking around causing a leak when their backs were turned. Earl parked Emily's car. Leaving it parked on the road was also a risk. Some homeowners had nothing else to do but spy through their windows with more diligence than Santa maintaining his list of naughty or nice, eager to report the slightest infraction to the president of the homeowner's association.

"We're with you, Keith," encouraged Earl.

They walked up the driveway to the elaborate cherry-wood door with an oval finished-glass inset with intricate designs. Earl rang the doorbell and sensed Keith move behind Emily and him out of the line of sight. After about a minute, the door opened. Richard looked tired, gone was the fire that was in his eyes the night he drove Earl from the church.

"What are you doing here?" came a gruff but weaker than normal voice.

Earl mustered confidence for Keith's sake. "I've brought someone to see you."

Keith slowly stepped from behind Earl and Emily. His voice was thick with emotion as he spoke. "I hope I'm welcome, dad. Pastor Earl said I would be … Am I?"

Richard's body trembled with emotion. Tears welled in his eyes and rolled softly down the crevasses in his face. "My son." His voice was barely a breath, and it carried the weight of a decade of heartache. He held open his arms, shaking as though he were seeing an apparition that could vanish at any moment, and Keith stepped in. Richard hugged him tightly, his body heaving from sobs. "After all these years, you've come home," his words muffled against Keith's shoulder. They stood for what seemed like minutes, clinging to each other as though sharing a decade's worth of separate memories and losses within that short span of time. Finally, Richard held Keith at arms' length to get a good look at him. "Welcome home." A smile broke through the tears, and Keith mirrored the smile. Richard glanced around at the others standing there. "And who is this pretty, young lady?"

"This is Emily. She's my girlfriend."

"I'm pleased to meet you, Emily. Now, everyone come in." Richard put his arm around Keith and Emily and ushered them inside.

Earl stood watching and was about to turn around and head for the car when Richard's voice cut through his thoughts.

"After all I've said to you, and the way I treated you, you still brought my son home to me. Why?"

"It was the right thing to do."

"I still don't understand. You don't even like me."

Earl stood, wondering what to say. Then words came to him, as if by a gift and not really his own. "I've studied the Bible a lot. I don't recall Jesus commanding people to like each other, but he did command them to love each other."

Richard stared at Earl, blinking. "Come inside, Earl."

"Your son is home, Richard. Spend time catching up with him and getting to know Emily." Earl paused, shocked at the words that were about to come out of his mouth. "Merry Christmas, Richard."

Richard wore a shocked expression. Slowly, it became a smile, a smile that Earl had never seen Richard give him before.

Richard closed the door, but Earl could still hear his excitement through it. Earl walked about halfway down the driveway and stopped. He stood there, paralyzed and lost in thought. Then something astonishing happened. He knew no other way to describe it. It was as if a wall that had enclosed his mind began crumbling, bit by bit, until it crashed into dust. He hadn't seen this plainly in years. Harmony was right. He had not believed the very message he preached. And he knew why Keith's situation spoke so strongly to him. He and Keith were essentially the same.

They got by, but they were emotionally broken. Earl had been like a shard of pottery. It was good at scooping rice or solid food, but it was ill-equipped for liquid. He did God's business, but only to a certain extent. God didn't want him to be a shard of pottery. God wanted to use a whole bowl. Earl had been fighting God for years. He was trying to be content being a shard of pottery. He had wondered why God had forsaken him, but he was the one who had forsaken God. What was so strange was that people had been telling him that, but he chose not to see it. He chose to hang on to his guilt. God didn't want his guilt; he wanted his repentance. "What am I doing? If Keith could get the courage to see his father after such a long time, surely, I can face my lack of confidence." It had taken seeing someone else have the courage to face his fears head-on for Earl to realize that was what he needed to do. He couldn't run away. He didn't know if the church would let him stay, but he had to have the courage to find out.

Earl pulled out his phone and pulled up the messaging app the church used. He recorded a message. "Everyone who can, please come to the church tonight at seven p.m. If you know of people who aren't part of the automated messaging system, let them know. This is very important." Earl sent the message. Now, he needed to exchange Emily's car for his own and get back to the parsonage.

At precisely seven o'clock that evening, Earl, unsure of his fate, walked confidently into the church. He had not paid attention to the cars in the parking lot. Had he, he would not have been surprised to see every church pew filled with parishioners, many more than were usually present for the Sunday service. The Church Council sat on the center front pew. The air stirred with the chatter of people wondering what was so urgent. Earl walked to the pulpit and the chatter ceased. All attention was on Earl.

"Thank you for coming tonight. During my first appointment at Pinewood Church, I concentrated on community outreach so much that the Church Council had me reappointed to another church because I didn't focus on the congregation. My confidence in doing community outreach was shattered because I believed I had failed the church. So, I turned to preaching instead and avoided outreach as much as possible. This year, the bishop sent me back here to face this church and regain my confidence. Instead, I fell into the same trap as before, doing things instead of focusing on you. Even when I involved others, it was primarily others outside of this church."

Jerry spoke up so that all could hear. "But that's the Christian thing to do, help the community."

"You're right Jerry, but I've realized that to focus on the congregation and on community outreach, I have to work with you so that we do it together. When we help others together, we help ourselves. I heard that message a few weeks ago from an eight-year-old girl, but it didn't really sink in. Because I didn't realize that until today, we didn't come close to reaching our fund drive goal, and I damaged a relationship with Farmer Brown, who was trying to help us. I'm here tonight to ask for your forgiveness and your help in the next few days to reach our goal."

The congregation was quiet. People glanced around at each other as if trying to see what others were thinking or what the right response was. Earl knew they had probably not received this amount of candidness before from a minister. The Church Council seemed the same. Ted Long's face seemed to reflect his torn thoughts on the matter. But no one was speaking. Finally, a man in the very back pew stood up. It was Richard Coldwell. With a voice of authority, a voice with newfound strength, he proclaimed, "Well, what do you say people? Are we going to forgive our pastor and help him or what?"

Earl was floored to see Richard there. But Richard's questions opened the floodgates. The sanctuary was buzzing with conversation. Then, one person in the middle of the sanctuary stood up and said, "I forgive you, Pastor, and I'll help in any way I can." One by one, every person in the church stood and did the same.

With everyone still standing, Ted stepped out from the pew and faced the congregation. "While we're all here, let's decide what we can do to try to meet our goal. I suppose it's too late to sell Christmas trees."

Terrence, a father of four teen boys, addressed the group. "I've got four strong boys who can unload and set up the trees. I'm sure there are still a few people who haven't bought trees yet."

"But are there enough people who haven't bought one yet to allow us to reach our goal?" reminded Ted.

Peggy, a parishioner who was normally very quiet spoke out. "It might be too late to sell trees for people's homes, but what if we set up trees on the church property to form sort of parade of trees? People could buy one and then decorate their tree. People might want to buy them in memory of a loved one or to honor someone.

They could decorate their tree, and we could provide signs for them to write who the tree is dedicated to. That way, they could come when they wanted to to visit the tree and remember the person."

Several people liked the idea and voiced their support.

"But what would we do for decorations?" asked Ted. The trees would look very plain without any decorations at all."

"People may more than likely want to personalize their tree with their own decorations," declared Peggy.

Another parishioner, Tabia, said, "There are plenty of pinecones in the woods on the outskirts of town, and we can always string popcorn."

Melvin, the hardware store owner, added, "I overpurchased bird seed that I was going to get rid of. I'll donate that for ornaments."

Someone else yelled out, "For those of us who aren't crafty, we could always just ask for donations."

Mai, who ran the bakery, announced, "I'll donate ten percent of all my bakery sales the next few days."

Maria, one of the Church Councilwomen, spoke next. "I heard talk of serving a meal for the mobile home community and that Victorious Life Church was willing to help. Are we still going to do that? If so, we need to contact the local eateries for help with the food."

"Ok. Let's organize this," stated Earl. "Everyone who is willing to do these different jobs can gather in groups and make plans."

The sanctuary was filled with conversations, shouts of where a particular group was, and laughter, as people began to move to different areas of the sanctuary to make plans. Some groups made plans to meet the next day. Others stayed and made plans while people were still there. After about an hour-and-a-half, the last of the people began to leave.

Earl thought everyone had gone when Richard walked up to him. "I imagine you were surprised to see me here tonight," hinted Richard.

Earl had whipped around at Richard's voice, and shock momentarily showed on his face. "I admit that I was."

"After all of the things I said to you, did to you, you still found it in your heart to convince my son to come home to me. I need to ask forgiveness from you."

"You have it." And Earl meant it with all his heart.

Richard clasped Earl on the shoulder. "You're going to be all right, Pastor."

"How do you know that?"

Richard smiled a knowing smile. "Because you've finally forgiven yourself."

Jerry stopped by the church the next day, and Earl took the opportunity to pin him down about the three gifts. He was sure that

Jerry was behind the gifts. "Come on, Jerry, fess up. It was you behind the three gifts, right?"

"Not me," he replied casually.

"It has to be. Emily called almost immediately after I left the parsonage on Tuesday. You were the only one who knew the exact time I left, and Emily said that you told her to call me."

"That doesn't prove it was me."

"If it wasn't, then you know who is."

"Maybe. Maybe not. What I am sure of is that I'm glad you decided to come back. What you did took a tremendous amount of courage. I'm proud of you."

Chapter Twenty-Four

Over the next several days, the church was busy. Usually, this was a time when people focused on their families and getting ready for Christmas themselves. What Earl witnessed was truly a miracle that only God could have inspired in people.

Terrence and Jerry helped Farmer Brown cut the trees. Once they explained what had happened in the church on Tuesday night, Farmer Brown teared up and donated all of the trees they needed. Terrence and his four sons did the heavy lifting of loading, transporting, and setting up the trees in the churchyard. Another group had marked where each tree should go to leave enough room among the trees and to create a walking path through the trees.

Others advertised in town and made calls to inform people what the church was doing. Rather than setting the hours from five o'clock to eight o'clock, people took shifts so that at least one person was there the entire day. Soon, townsfolk came out and purchased trees. They were able to pick out the tree they wanted along the path. There were different sizes of trees to allow for different amounts of decorations. Peggy was at the churchyard all day, almost every day, and she provided signs for people to write the names for memorials and honorariums.

There were a variety of decorations. Jerry had three large crates of deer apples that a few people in the congregation sliced, dried, and tied biodegradable cotton thread to. Several of the youth in the church strung popcorn for garland. Children in the congregation used peanut butter and bird seed on pinecones to make ornaments. Others brought their own decorations for a personable touch. A young woman decorated a tree in memory of her late grandfather, using a photo of him fishing along with fishing lures, his fishing pole, and his fishing hat. A young man decorated a tree in memory of his late mother using spools of thread, thimbles, a sewing machine ornament, yarn, a needlepoint design, a crocheted scarf, and photos of her sewing and crafting. A wife decorated a tree in honor of her husband who was an auto technician. She used miniature car models and car parts. Richard, Keith, and Emily bought and decorated a tree in memory of Ms. Coldwell. They used pictures that were used at her celebration of life ceremony. It was a way for Keith to come to terms with missing his mother's funeral. Luis and the other youth from the mobile home neighborhood purchased a tree as well. One of the teens sold his pair of autographed shoes that was given to him by Jarrett Bridges so that they would have enough money to buy the tree. The group didn't dedicate the tree to a specific person. Instead, they decorated it with a myriad of objects, photos of parents and grandparents, objects that were special to people, photos with Jarrett Bridges, and even a photo of Earl. The trees were as unique as the people they represented, but it all worked to create a beautiful and inspiring reflection trail. And people not only focused on their own trees, they looked at many of the others in testament to the value of each person.

Earl bought a tree to dedicate to the history of Pinewood Church, especially its history at its former location. He called Monk, the owner of Churchdale Barbeque, who had the stone transported and set beside of the tree. Earl and Jerry looked through the archives, and Earl copied pictures, old church bulletins, and whatever else he could find. The tree turned out to be one of the more popular trees on the tree walk.

The second night the tree was displayed, Hank and Elaine Waters stopped by, to Earl's surprise.

"We heard that you dedicated a tree to the former church building," inquired Hank.

"It's true," answered Earl.

"Why?" quizzed Hank.

"We know that the old church was a painful reminder of your previous time in Pinewood," added Elaine.

"It was for me, but I realized, primarily talking with you, that the old church building held a special place in many congregants' hearts. They deserved to be able to remember the old building with fondness. Plus, dedicating the tree was therapeutic for me, and I imagine it could be therapeutic for others as well."

"Would you take us to see it?" inquired Hank.

"Of course," replied Earl. Earl took the Waters to see the tree. Tears welled in Hank's eyes as he studied the decorations on the tree. Then he got down on both knees next to the stone and rubbed his fingers across the name, *Waters*.

"How did you find the stone?" asked Hank. "I thought it had been thrown away."

"The owner of Churchdale Barbeque apparently offered it to the church, but a former pastor didn't want it. I'm sure it wasn't presented to the Church Council. If it had been, I'm sure they would have voted to accept it. He didn't want to dispose of it; so, he decided to keep and store it."

"I'm glad he saved it." Hank paused. A question stuck hard in his throat, and it took at least half a minute to ask. "I have a favor to ask. "I've finished the scale model of the church. Would it be ok with you if we set the model next to the tree, and would you keep in in the church after Christmas?"

"I'd be glad to have it set up beside of the tree. I'll speak to the Church Council about putting it in the church. I won't make any promises, but I imagine they will be more than happy to accept it."

Hank had the model in his vehicle, and several people helped transport it from Hank's vehicle to the tree.

"This is beautiful!" exclaimed Earl. "The details are amazing. Even the church pews inside the model are truly remarkable." Earl did a double take at the windows in the model. The windows were stained glass that were a scaled down version of the stained-glass windows that had adorned the actual church. "The stained-glass windows are exceptional, true works of art."

Elaine cast a glance to the top of the tree. "Why do you have a cross at the top rather than a star?"

Earl smiled. "Isaiah 53:5 states, *But he was wounded for our transgressions; he was bruised for our iniquities; upon him was the chastisement that brought us peace, and by his stripes we are healed.* The star points to the promise of redemption. The cross is the realization of that redemption. We are a church in need of healing and redemption. This verse reminds us that we have it through Christ's crucifixion. I thought the cross was an appropriate tree topper for that reason."

Both Hank and Elaine were silenced at the revelation. They quietly studied the tree for several more minutes before turning and walking away. Something told Earl that this palpable reminder of the old church had had a profound effect on both of them.

The reflection walk wasn't the only thing the church did to raise the money needed. Several people from the church went to stores and received donations of money from people for the toy drive. Mai, as promised, set aside money in a jar from each sale that week.

Maria, Earl, and several parishioners, including parishioners from Victorious Life Church visited local eateries to ask about donating prepared food for the mobile home neighborhood for a Christmas Day meal. In addition, many others heard about the meal and volunteered to help with cooking.

With a few days to go before Christmas, the church realized their goal and purchased the toys from the list that was given to Earl. An *all call* went out that night for people to come the next day and wrap toys. Both experienced and inexperienced gift wrappers showed up. Several of the experienced gift wrappers took time to teach those who were not as talented in that area. Within a short time, all the presents had been wrapped. The remaining group of organizers laid out the plan for distributing the gifts by the day before Christmas Eve.

The day before Christmas Eve, Ted visited Earl in the Pinewood Church Office. "I was skeptical, but we've got all the presents that we needed wrapped, and tomorrow is Christmas Eve."

"Miracles have a way of happening at Christmas," exclaimed Earl. "All we have to do now is deliver the toys, and we have forty volunteers who will make the deliveries today."

"I've never told you this Earl, but I'm glad for our sake and for yours that the bishop saw fit to send you here."

Chapter Twenty-Five

Christmas Eve had arrived. Earl was starting to become a little more relaxed. They had raised the money for the toy drive and saved face with Farmer Brown. He needed to preach the sermon tonight at Victorious Life Church, and the Christmas meal at the mobile home neighborhood was tomorrow. Then he could rest, at least temporarily.

Earl pulled into the parking lot at Victorious Life Church. He was running slightly later than he wanted, but he had still arrived in plenty of time. He paused temporarily at the live nativity scene. A large crowd viewed the live nativity. The scene was spectacular. The stable was constructed from rough-hewn wood. Members of Victorious Life, from children to adults, played the various roles in authentic-looking costumes, Joseph, Mary with the baby Jesus, shepherds, angels, the three wise men, the little drummer boy, and even villagers. Of course, Farmer Brown had supplied the animals and bays of hay. He had sheep and two donkeys. Between helping both Pinewood Church and Victorious Life Church, Earl wondered how he got his farm work done.

Earl looked at his watch and tore himself away from the nativity scene. He made his way into the sanctuary, which was magnificently decorated for Christmas with poinsettias, holly, ivy, and mistletoe. People were already starting to come inside and sit. Earl spotted William at the front and rushed to meet him.

"Change of plans, Earl," exclaimed William. I'm going to deliver the message tonight. Have a seat here in the first row. William directed him to the front row of chairs.

"Alright." Earl was bewildered. He wondered if he had done something wrong or something to upset William. Or maybe William just changed his mind. It was his church after all. Now wasn't the time to talk about it, but he would try to catch him after the service. Earl sat next to Jerry. Luis and a few of his friends were also in the front row. After a few minutes the church was filled with people, most eagerly talking about the live nativity scene that they viewed outside.

William walked to the pulpit and surveyed the crowd, and he stood quietly for several seconds until the crowd grew quiet. The thought struck Earl that he had not seen William preach before. He wished he had taken the time to do so. He was impressed by William's presence and the authority in his posture. Although, he had yet to hear a single word of any of William's sermons, he sensed that the young man was an exceptional preacher. He would have to be in order for Victorious Life Church to have grown the way it had in the short amount of time since its inception.

The crowd had quieted, and William began. "I've got a story to tell tonight. It's not a traditional Christmas sermon. It's not about Bethlehem, a Christmas star, shepherds in the field, angels, a manger, or magi. But it is about why Jesus came to this world. It's about reconciliation and redemption." William paused and looked at Earl. "Most of you don't know that I grew up in Pinewood. I was from a poor family, and we lived in what people pejoratively called a trailer park. My life was headed for nowhere, like most of the youth who lived there. Then, one day, a new preacher, fresh out of seminary, came to Pinewood to preach at the most prestigious church in town. Now, we didn't care about preachers. They stayed in the church and wouldn't dare come to the trailer park. They might have preached about going to the poor, the disenfranchised, the ones everyone had forgotten, but words were the extent of it. But this new preacher came to us. He talked with us, expecting nothing in return. He taught some people how to play the guitar, others how to do first aid, others art, and so on. He visited the sick and elderly and held bingo games. Oh, to have seen the look on a senior's face when this preacher handed them a prize for winning at bingo was a sight more beautiful than the decorations in this church. One night, I was standing at the church with a rock in my hand and broken stained glass at my feet, and the pastor was driven away. I had just picked up the rock unknowingly, and people thought I threw the rock and broke the windows. Later, it came to light that someone else had broken the windows. But I still felt that the church was ruined because of me. It took me years to learn how to make stained glass, but I kept at it until I had made the stained-glass windows to replace the broken ones. You can see them now at Churchdale Barbeque, and I made the one here behind me. People are sometimes like stained glass, broken and colored with the worry of life's struggles, but God can take those colorful shards and put them together to make a beautiful creation. I went to a Bible College so that I, too, could be like this young preacher. He made a difference in my life that I can never repay." William walked from the pulpit to Earl. He pulled him up from his chair and hugged him. "Pastor Earl ... that's your third Christmas gift."

Earl waited until the crowd of people emptied the church. He was still in shock. He had no clue that William was the kid with the rock in his hand, the kid who had occupied his nightmares. Until Richard told him that Keith and friends of Keith had broken the windows, Earl had always thought that the kid with the rock was the final straw in his downfall. What a burden that had put on William. Earl couldn't believe how selfish he had been. In a few weeks' time he learned that Keith, William, and even Richard had suffered because of that night. Yet, William had overcome his guilt, just as Earl should have. Earl realized he didn't need to feel guilty that William found redemption and reconciliation before he had. He didn't need to trade one guilt for another. That was the thing about guilt. There were always multiple traps. You could escape one only to fall into another. The important thing was everyone scarred by that night had found forgiveness and redemption.

William reappeared in the sanctuary with a smile on his face.

"I'm sorry I didn't recognize you sooner," lamented Earl.

"You weren't expecting me. Besides, I'm not the same kid you knew back then. A decade has passed."

"Are you the one behind the three gifts?

"Yes. Remember, I was there when Richard Coldwell criticized you that night. I saw the pain on your face. I saw that same pain when you came back here. And I understood it. I felt a lot of that pain myself, but I knew the people whose lives you changed."

"Why didn't you tell me who you were?"

"I didn't want to be the kid with the rock in your eyes. I wanted you to see the impact you had on others' lives in order for you to see the impact you had on mine. I made a mistake though. I thought what you needed was to see the impact you had made. I didn't find out until about a week ago what you really needed to heal."

"You didn't make a mistake. Without your gifts, I wouldn't have seen what I needed to see to finally make me realize how to move past that night."

A thought entered Earl's mind, and he had to ask William another question. "The model church that Hank Waters made had stained-glass windows in it. At the time, I didn't think about who made those. Did you make those?"

"I did, and I owe that to you."

"How is that?"

"Remember that I called you when you were taking Harmony to Knoxville to see the Christmas Play. During that conversation, you mentioned that Mr. Waters was creating a scale model of the church. I paid him a visit and asked if he had stained-glass windows for the model. He didn't, and he was stuck, unable to finish the model. I volunteered to make them. He gladly accepted my offer, and fortunately, I had time to make them."

"Your gifts never stop. How can I ever repay you?"

"You did that a long time ago!"

Chapter Twenty-Six

Christmas night at the mobile home neighborhood was a sight to behold. Tents were set up with tables holding food from the Mainstreet Diner, Churchdale Barbeque, the bakery, and others, including food from individuals. The smell from meats, vegetables, and baked goods was an olfactory overload. Earl still couldn't get over the sacrifices that people made on Christmas Day to help others outside of their families. Earl, William, and parishioners from both churches helped serve food to the crowd gathered from the mobile home neighborhood. Carolers from both churches sang Christmas Carols.

Sunday morning, for the first time since being in Pinewood, Earl dressed in his pulpit robe and stole. He didn't know why he had not dressed in it sooner. Maybe he had not felt worthy. The Advent season was a perfect time to shed that feeling.

"The first sermon I tried to preach when I arrived back here at Pinewood Church was the Prodigal Son. From all that's happened during the last week, I think it is fitting that I try that sermon again. There have been so many truths in this parable, and I've preached almost every one of them. But I only recently learned a new truth, one that should have been obvious. We all know that Jesus showed us the picture of God as a father, a loving, providing, and forgiving father who will keep giving us chances to reconcile with him. But notice that Jesus didn't tell us what happened to the brothers. It makes us wonder. Did they forgive each other, tolerate each other, or completely disassociate from each other? Do you wonder why Jesus didn't tell us what happened? It's because the ending is up to us. Good and bad happen to us all. We hurt each other whether we mean to or not. We choose whether to give our fellow brothers and sisters another chance. The end of the story is up to us. I was given some gifts that have healed a hurt I carried within me for years. Giving and receiving is so fundamental that God reminds us of it constantly. He gave us our first breath; we gave that breath back to the world. Every time we breathe, it's a reminder to receive and to give. Hopefully, it is a reminder to give forgiveness and second chances."

After the worship service, Earl greeted parishioners, as usual, as they exited the church. Richard, Keith, and Emily were all smiles as they advanced toward Earl.

"Pastor," beamed Keith. "Emily has agreed to marry me!"

"That's wonderful! Congratulations to you both!"

"We want you to perform the wedding ceremony," added Keith.

"I'd be honored. I'm supposed to leave at the end of June though. When were you wanting to get married?"

"I know this seems like a rush," admitted Emily, "but we want Mr. Coldwell to be well enough to attend."

"Please call me, dad, or at least Richard," he interjected.

"We were hoping within the next week or two."

Earl didn't seem shocked by the answer. He sort of expected it. "As long as you're sure, there's no reason why we can't perform the ceremony within that time frame. The main thing is getting a marriage license. Do you know where you want the ceremony?"

"We do," they replied in unison with tentativeness in their voices. Keith and Emily turned their attention to Richard.

"They would like to have it at Churchdale Barbeque. Part of the reason is that Emily works there, and Keith plays there occasionally. The other reason is that they thought getting married there would close one turbulent chapter of our lives and issue in a new chapter where there could be good memories."

"I think that is a good reason. I'd be happy to perform the ceremony there."

As the line was nearing its end, Earl stole a glance to see how many people were left. He was shocked to see Harmony's parents at the very end of the line. He had not seen them during the service. As was his practice, he had surveyed the entire congregation at some point during the sermon. Of course, he had not seen Richard in the congregation the night he asked the church for forgiveness; so, he knew there were some blind spots in the church. Perhaps Hank and Elaine Waters were sitting in one of those spots. By the time Hank and Elaine reached Earl, they were the only ones left in the sanctuary.

"It's good to see you again!" exclaimed Earl. "Thank you for coming out today."

Elaine was fidgety and appeared nervous as she began to speak. "Hank and I have been talking and we'd like to rededicate our membership here."

"That would be wonderful," replied Earl. "I have to admit that I'm curious though. A couple of weeks ago, coming back to church here didn't seem like a possibility. What has changed?"

"I think we each wanted our own thing and couldn't compromise," answered Hank. "I know a person can't go back in time. The old location, as a church, is probably gone forever, but I wanted to hear it acknowledged for what it meant to people. In moving to this location, it seemed easily dismissed. What you did with the founder's stone, dedicating the Christmas Tree, and getting the model I built put in this church showed me that someone cared. I think I'm finally ready to move on."

"We also doing this because we're afraid our inability to compromise may have negatively impacted Harmony," added Elaine.

Earl dropped his head from the weight of Harmony's name in his mind. "I really miss Harmony. How is she?"

"She really misses you a lot too," soothed Elaine. "Because we couldn't compromise, we're afraid she was trying too hard to find a compromise with you when one didn't really exist."

"She told us what happened," interjected Hank. "I don't think there was anything you could do that would have worked except to have gone to Philadelphia with her. But I don't see how that could have worked either. Even if you could convince the bishop to send you there, after a few years, you would be relocated again. Then you would be right back in the same spot as you are now. Harmony loves you. I wish it could have all worked out. I hate to see her going through life alone."

"Thank you for telling me that. I've tried to call Harmony a few times, but she hasn't taken my calls. I'm afraid I've blown it for sure with her this time." Earl paused to concentrate on putting a smile on his face. "Well, I'm glad you want to rededicate your membership. I'll be the best pastor I can."

Chapter Twenty-Seven

Earl had been so busy that he had not had a chance to talk with the bishop. He had sent him a Christmas Card, but he yearned to talk with Chris. Finally, after Christmas, Earl called Chris. He told Chris about Harmony, the three gifts, and his Damascene moment. Earl had prayed about his assignment and felt led to make a request of the bishop.

"I don't think I'm hearing you correctly, Earl. You want to give up the megachurch in Dallas and stay at Pinewood?"

"For a couple of years anyway. I want to have the opportunity to build up the church. And working with Pastor William Lorie, I think we can help strengthen the community.

"To be honest," hesitated Chris, "I doubted the decision to send you to Pinewood a few times myself. Sometimes, it's difficult to understand why we need to take a rough road when we know there is an easier route available, but God has a plan and a purpose, even if it is not always obvious to us. But never in my wildest dreams did I expect to hear what you've told me. To be honest, I was thinking of bringing you back in January. I thought that one or two months would give you the opportunity to face your fears. I still can't believe my ears to hear that you want to stay longer. It's been your dream to be a televangelist. Are you certain you want to give that dream up?"

"I'm not saying I'm giving up on it forever. I just feel that Pinewood is a better place for me now."

"I'll grant your request. By the way, how many gifts did the letter tell you that you would receive?"

"Three."

"From all you've said, I think you received way more than three."

"God gives abundantly."

After Earl hung up, he thought about Harmony. He knew he had received so much already, but he couldn't help but wish he had received that gift as well. Then, he remembered his sermon on the prodigal son. The father had given his son even more gifts than the son expected. The father seemed to have a never-ending abundance. God did have a never-ending abundance of gifts to give.

On January first, Earl was at Chuchdale Barbeque to perform the wedding ceremony of Keith Coldwell and Emily Davis. Churchdale Barbeque was closed for the wedding. It was a small intimate ceremony. Richard, William, the owner of Churchdale, members of the band, and a few others were in attendance. The violinist from the band played a variation of Pachelbel's Canon in D as Emily walked down the aisle. At the end of the ceremony, Earl pronounced the couple husband and wife. Keith and Emily kissed, and Richard hugged the newly married couple. Keith and Emily had not planned to go anywhere on their honeymoon. The band had some gigs set up, and Emily's last semester in nursing school started in a couple of weeks. Richard offered to pay for Emily's last semester so that she wouldn't have to have a job while attending nursing school. Although she objected, Richard insisted and wouldn't take *no* for an answer until she finally relented.

Chapter Twenty-Eight

In an office in a high-rise building in Philadelphia, Harmony Waters sat behind her desk. Her face was illuminated by the light from the dual computer monitors at which she stared. She lowered her head and scrunched up her eyes as she massaged the corners of her eyes with her thumb and forefinger.

A knock on her open door caused her to look over and find her administrative assistant standing there with a fretful look on her face.

"Ms. Waters, I'm sorry for the interruption, but someone is insisting on seeing you. He looks harmless enough, but I can call security and have him escorted out if you wish."

"No. Send him in. I'll see him."

The administrative assistant notified Earl that Harmony would see him. He furtively approached Harmony's office door and peered in. Harmony was still staring at her monitors, almost as if she had already forgotten that someone was coming in to see her. Earl had an angular view of Harmony, and even that was partially obstructed by furniture and office technology, but catching sight of her was pure heaven. Almost two months had passed since he had seen Harmony. He missed her tremendously; actually, that was understating it. He ached to see Harmony. He was better and stronger emotionally than he ever had been, yet something still didn't feel quite right yet. His soul might be healed, but he had a hole in his heart that needed mending. With God's strength, he could get by without Harmony, but he didn't want to have to. His life felt so much more enriched, so much more blessed with her in it.

Earl stood in the doorway, taking Harmony in, like a man who had spent days in the desert taking in water. She must have remembered that someone was coming to see her, either that or she felt someone's presence looking at her. She almost jumped in her seat when she spied Earl. Surprise effused over her face.

"May I come in?" asked Earl.

Harmony's face seemed to be in a tug of war. One side appeared to want to run to him, hold and kiss him. The other side appeared to play aloof and cautious. He didn't know which side would win out. Even if the aloofness won, would that be a true indication of how she felt or merely a guise to keep her emotionally safe?

"Please do. I have to say that I'm surprised to see you, pleasantly surprised, but surprised. What are you doing here?" Harmony moved from behind the desk and cautiously approached Earl. She reached up without touching him with her hands and kissed him on the cheek.

Not a good sign, thought Earl. Earl felt he needed to act quickly before Harmony's position became set against his favor; so, he launched into his rehearsed plea. "I made a mess of things when you left, and I've come to hopefully make amends."

Harmony's steely eyes cut into Earl's soul like a sharp knife through warm butter. "I think you were pretty clear when I left."

The deck felt stacked against Earl, but he had to try. "That's the thing. I wasn't clear. You were right about me needing more than one gift. It took the courage of Keith Coldwell for me to have enough faith and courage to take a risk. I realized that I had made the same mistake twice. I asked for the church's forgiveness and help, and I received both. I finally saw that I could help the Pinewood congregation and the community by involving the congregation in the outreach. I convinced the bishop to let me stay on in Pinewood for a couple of years to help strengthen both the church and the community."

"Keith Coldwell? Richard's son?"

Earl explained the whole sequence of events following Harmony's departure. He couldn't read any telltale signs on her face as he related the story to her.

"That warms my heart to hear that you've healed, but why are you here?"

"Because I now have the courage to tell you that I not only love you but I'm willing to do what it takes to win you back, if it's not too late. We had something special, and I don't want to give it up without trying. I know life's moved on for both of us, but if we both love each other, we can make it work. I still love you."

Wistful eyes spoke volumes, but her words confirmed what her eyes indicated. "I wish you could have come to that conclusion earlier. We could have made a plan."

"We still can."

"Can we?"

"Less than a couple of months has passed. Whatever plan we could have come up with at the time, we can still do. If you no longer love me, I'll accept the consequences of my inaction."

"It was never a question of love."

If Harmony's decision was made, begging wouldn't help. He told her how he felt. He made the first effort since she left. If that wasn't enough to win her heart, then he didn't know what else would. "I've laid my feelings on the line. This is a two-way street, and the ball's in your court. You know how to reach me. I'm not going to stand here and try to force an answer."

"Good-bye, Earl."

Well, that was the answer. Earl felt like kicking himself for not trying when he had the chance. Perhaps that was the real reason for her answer, he thought. Maybe Harmony felt like this was an afterthought. If he could not have taken the chance when he was given it, she didn't want to take it now. Maybe she thought that Earl needed her rather than wanted her. Maybe she thought he was coming from a place of weakness now. Maybe. Maybe. What may have been was in the past. The present was what counted now, and for whatever reason, she felt differently now than she had in the past. "Good-bye, Harmony."

The disappointing finale with Harmony weighed heavily on Earl the next few months. He finally felt settled in one area of his life, only to realize that he was missing something in another area. Not having an intimate relationship with someone had never bothered Earl in the past. Yet, a few weeks of knowing Harmony had made Earl acutely aware of what he had been missing. It seemed strange to Earl how a few weeks could shape an entire life. But he supposed that was the way life always was. One bad decision could ruin or even end a life. One good decision could birth happiness that would last for a lifetime. Split second decisions in a present moment could make or break the present moments in one's life. Earl wondered if that was really sound thinking. Wasn't there choice in each present moment? He supposed there was, but previous moments could make choice either easier or more difficult in other present moments. That was where faith in God came into play. Not to change the past but to help one deal with the present. And deal with it, Earl did. Whenever he felt the sting of regret, of lost hope, he leaned into God, the God who had helped turn his life around. And God could do the same here, if Earl would let him.

Earl dug into his vision of rebuilding Pinewood Church and working with William to help strengthen the community. Like Ebenezer Scrooge, Earl wanted to be better than his word. He involved the congregation in every activity, capitalizing on others' talents to help. Things seemed to come much easier, and he felt better than he ever had when it came to doing God's work. Of course, at his previous church he relied on a few others to do things he didn't want to do, but this was different. He wasn't taking advantage of anyone to benefit himself. He was partnering with others so that all could benefit, those helping and those receiving help.

Pinewood and Victorious Life churches jointly planned a Christmas in July event to be held on a Saturday during the third week of July. Certain events were planned for the morning at Pinewood Church, and other events were planned at Victorious Life Church from one p.m. to ten p.m. Transportation was set up to transport people from Pinewood Church to Victorious Life Church. There was also transportation from select locations to the churches and then back to those locations throughout the day.

Earl went up to the outdoor stage to start the events at Pinewood Church. A huge banner that read *Christmas in July* hung over his head. Christmas music played in the background through numerous speakers that had been set up. Although more people would come throughout the day, there was already a good-sized crowd that had gathered. The day was already warm, a preamble to the hot day that lay ahead. As Earl spoke, the speakers boomed Earl's voice like summer thunder. "Thank you for coming out to celebrate Christmas in July. Victorious Life and Pinewood churches have put together this day with events at both churches. We'll start here with Christmas Bingo, games, the Christmas-themed summer treats contest, the dress like summer Santa contest, and a learn to make Christmas crafts session. Then transportation will be provided to Victorious Life Church where we'll have a Christmas-themed potluck lunch around one o'clock, more Christmas games, and a holiday movie. I'd also like to make an announcement. Pinewood and Victorious Life churches have set up a fund for disadvantaged or impoverished families in Pinewood to allow youth to stay in school. We are calling it RISE, which stands for Reach, Invest, Support, and Educate. We have an information booth if you would like to learn more. Let the fun begin."

People sprinted to activities like runners at the sound of the start gun. Earl couldn't help but laugh at the excitement that spread through the crowd like a contagion. As Earl stepped down from the stage, William strode up to him.

"I think over half the crowd are people from the community," suggested William. "Hopefully, that will help get information out about the RISE fund. By the way, the local bank will use some of its foundation funds to support this effort."

"All of that is wonderful news. We wanted to bring the churches and community together. Hopefully, this is just the beginning."

While Earl and William were talking, Richard, Keith, and Emily walked over.

"Earl, William!" greeted Richard. "I wanted to share the good news that Emily has finished her nursing program and will start work at the hospital next week."

Earl hugged Emily. "That's wonderful news! Congratulations, Emily!"

Keith and Emily left in search of one of the activities while Richard stayed behind.

"I also wanted to share some personal news with you," declared Richard. "With the new treatments I was put on, the doctor says the cancer is in remission."

Earl clasped Richard's hand firmly. "I prayed for that, Richard. I'm so happy to hear that."

Richard beamed. "Any amount of additional time I have with Keith and Emily is a blessing. I think my improved health has been as much about forgiveness and letting go as the medical treatments. Thank you, Earl." Richard clapped Earl on the shoulder, and he headed after Keith and Emily.

William snuck a short distance away to give Earl and Richard some privacy while they spoke. He glided back over to Earl, who looked up to see William wearing a mischievous grin.

"I have a surprise for you, Earl."

"Not more gifts!"

William gave an undecipherable smile that left Earl wondering whether there was another gift or not. As William grasped Earl's shoulders, Earl's insides stirred with anticipation while his mind clouded with confusion. Earl allowed himself to be turned around in clock-hand like movement. Awaiting him at the terminus of his movement was a smiling face that transformed him into mush. For a moment, all thought vanished from his fizzled brain, and his breath caught in his throat. Here he was, face-to-face with Harmony. Her eyes sparkled with a warmth he had not seen since December. The smile on her face radiated a brilliance that, to Earl, outshone the morning sun. The memories of her, which had been the only comfort Earl had, now fled from his mind as the real person stood before him. The excitement and noise from the crowd faded in the background, and it was as if just the two of them were alone in an electrifying moment of reconnection. He had prayed for a reunion, and not just for a meeting but for a lasting, permanent presence in his life and heart. The words he wanted to tell her escaped from his mind, and all that would come out was, "Harmony! You're here."

"Is that all you can say?" she answered wryly.

"It really is. I don't know how to say what I'm feeling."

"I hope that's a good sign." Her eyes sparkled with amusement at Earl's struggle.

Earl exhaled a breath that he didn't know he was holding. "It's a very good sign. I hope it's a good sign that you're here!"

"It is. I'm staying here for as long as you are. Philadelphia wasn't what I expected, mostly because you weren't there. I went to church there and Jarrett Bridges belonged to that church. We struck up a friendship, and Jarrett told me that no matter how talented you are, you don't thrive unless you're under the right conditions."

"That sounds like Jarrett. And if he said anything that even remotely brought you back to me, then that's the greatest gift he could ever give to me."

"He also told me to tell you he has gotten to know some baseball and football players well. He and the other players will be happy to come help any time."

"That's good news, but if that happens it won't be just me calling for a favor. The church here has to be involved."

"Well, I'm part of this church now."

Earl looked at her with incredulous eyes. He wanted to pinch himself to make sure he wasn't in a dream, but he knew that would look strange. Earl was in ecstasy. He couldn't budge the smile that took root on his face, and he didn't want to. He tingled and bubbled so much that he felt he couldn't contain it, but he didn't know what to do with his emotions. He grabbed her and held her tightly to him like a child holding a teddy bear.

"Ok. I can't breathe." Her voice struggled. "I really believe you're excited to see me. You're proving it!"

Earl let up on the squeeze, but he didn't want to let go of her completely. "Are you really back to stay?" Although she had already told him, Earl sought additional verification. He almost regretted asking, in case he had misheard her before.

"I am."

"I've missed you so much. When I left Philadelphia, I thought I would never see you again. It seemed so final." Earl let go of her to look into her eyes.

The smile disappeared from her face, and Earl couldn't read the look. He wondered what she was thinking and what she was going to say.

A pained sigh lowered her shoulders. Her voice was thick with emotion as she spoke. "When you came to Philadelphia, I wanted to run to you then and there. I'm sorry I didn't, but I was so caught off guard. I put up a wall. Maybe I put it up because I was caught off guard, or maybe I put it up because I was afraid of getting hurt. I suppose I needed to be sure that you were telling the truth about being whole. The hurt you were living with kept you from truly living, and I needed a whole person. I also think that because my parents couldn't compromise on a church, I saw how it affected people. I was looking for a compromise, but in reality, I wasn't. Even though I said I would compromise, I really wanted what I wanted. I'm sorry. It wasn't fair to make you feel at fault when I was the one to blame. The main thing is, I love you. I never stopped loving you. I just needed to know that we had a future."

"I love you too. None of the other matters anymore as long as you're here. Not a day has gone by that I haven't thought about you. Although what Jarrett said may have helped, what made you realize that I was ready for you?"

"My parents are here, and I still have friends here. I've heard about the metamorphosis you've undergone. I realize that you learned what you needed to learn. I have too, and I have faith that we'll be ok."

"I thought Pinewood was my greatest curse. It's turning out to be my greatest blessing, especially since you're back."

Harmony caressed his face with her fingers. With each gentler touch, Earl felt the caress on his heartstrings, playing a tune that caused his heart to pound as his passion reached a crescendo. He cupped her cheek, his thumb lightly brushing her chin. Harmony closed her eyes and leaned in. Their faces were inches apart, and Earl could feel the warmth of her breach as it caressed his face. In eager anticipation, he tilted his head and closed his eyes. Their mouths parted as they traversed the few inches separating their waiting lips. Their lips met in a soft tentative kiss of rediscovery, almost an apology for missed moments. The kiss quickly yielded to the hope of moments to come as it deepened. Earl's hands found her lower back, and he gently pulled her even closer. Harmony's hands draped around Earl's neck. When he reluctantly pulled away, their foreheads gently rested against each other and their breaths mingled, creating a perfume of renewed dreams that lingered in the air around them. They smiled, knowing that a new shared chapter lay ahead of them. Whatever that was, and wherever that was, Pinewood had indeed become one of the greatest blessings in both of their lives.

About the Author

Dewey Dellinger is an educator and administrator. He was born, raised, and lives in North Carolina and has degrees from North Carolina State University, the University of North Carolina at Charlotte, and East Carolina University. His highest degree is a Ph.D. from North Carolina State University. His novel genres include fantasy, action-adventure, romance and romantic comedy, and drama.

Books by Dewey

Once Upon a Knight's Time Series

Once Upon a Knight's Time

Once Upon a Knight's Time: Seeker of the Sword

Romance

Love's Trail in Kenya

Romantic Comedy

Wrestling with Christmas

Action Heroine

Captain Tomorrow

Drama

Gifts to the Prodigal